THE
UNEARTHLY
TRAVAILS
OF GABRIEL MCGREGOR

THE
UNEARTHLY
TRAVAILS
OF GABRIEL MCGREGOR

BRAD ULREICH

TATE PUBLISHING
AND ENTERPRISES, LLC

Published by Tate Publishing & Enterprises, LLC
127 E. Trade Center Terrace | Mustang, Oklahoma 73064 USA
1.888.361.9473 | www.tatepublishing.com

Tate Publishing is committed to excellence in the publishing industry. The company reflects the philosophy established by the founders, based on Psalm 68:11,
"The Lord gave the word and great was the company of those who published it."

Book design copyright © 2014 by Tate Publishing, LLC. All rights reserved.
Cover design by Nikolai Purpura
Interior design by Jimmy Sevilleno

Published in the United States of America

ISBN: 978-1-63268-192-8
1. Fiction / Fantasy / Paranormal
2. Fiction / Occult & Supernatural
14.05.14

To Wendy
If it weren't for you, this book would be
but an unedited manuscript, still.

FATHER'S FORBIDDEN BASEMENT

GABRIEL MCGREGOR AWOKE that July morning as bright-eyed and bushy-tailed as any normal eleven-year-old boy would tend to awake in the summertime, but unfortunately for him, he ended that particular day, dead.

But even though Gabriel was normal, he was also quite an unusual boy. He was normal in the sense of having two arms, two legs, and one head, for instance, but unusual in having an intense curiosity about the workings of the universe on a level that worried his already-prone-to-worry mother.

He was normal in the sense of liking to eat when he was hungry, but unusual in that he really loved—no, *really loved*—to read thick, technical scientific tomes, many of the most fascinating in his possession he'd discovered in his deceased father's forbidden-to-enter and supposedly locked-up basement laboratory.

He was normal in regards to the fact that he slept when he was tired, but unusual because sometimes he'd spend days at a time awake, thinking through problems and divining solutions, and also exploring his father's basement laboratory, trying to figure what sense he could make out what seemed to be a multitude of inventions in various states of completion. One of the first real problems that he solved, actually, was how to crack the seven locks that his mother had installed on the door leading down to the basement, after his father had died.

Gabriel was only five years old at the time his dad had died, and his memories where blurred at best, but as soon as he realized that he wasn't supposed to go into the basement under any circumstances, and that the space beyond that door had something to do with his dead father—probably when he was seven years old or so—he made it his mission in life to pick those locks.

He was so clever about it, in fact, that his mother never noticed a thing. It soon became a habit of his to spend an entire evening or two down there each week, when he was supposedly sleeping in his bed, exploring his father's brain by way of exploring his forbidden workshop. He saw a lot of things that he didn't understand, but he was a quick learner, and fortunately for Gabriel, his father liked books, and had amassed a large library of them. There was a computer too, but as of yet, Gabriel hadn't deduced a password enabling a successful logon.

On that strange, bright summer morning, the slightly gangly, sharp-featured eleven-year-old Gabriel sat alight at the kitchen table, forking down some buttery pancakes. His brow-ridge creased in much more thought than a kid ought to be caught in. His five-year-old sister, Emma, sat across from him, flinging apple sauce into his brown hair. Ignoring the apple assault, it dawned on Gabriel to finally screw up the courage to ask his mom some serious questions about his departed dad.

She'd been cruelly silent about him, Gabriel felt, once he began to understand the concept of death better. He'd been Gabe's father, after all, and he didn't know anything about him, except for the fact that he was dead, and that his mom wasn't very forthcoming about the whole affair.

"Mom?"

"Yes, Gabe?"

Gabriel's mother—Susan McGregor—was a tall, handsome woman, with long, reddish-brown hair, and sharp features like Gabriel's. Her eyes gleamed intelligence. She was standing near the sink in her pink bathrobe and orange fuzzy slippers, tidying up the kitchen, and had fallen into one of her customary silent funks, no doubt mulling over something that was troubling her greatly, as this seemed to be her tendency. So there was a slightly annoyed twang to her voice, although Gabriel knew by now not to take this type of thing personally.

"What was Dad's job?" Gabriel asked, eyeing her a bit.

"I've already told you, Gabe...He worked for the government. A government employee. Nine to five." Mrs. McGregor was staring into the sink, not wanting to have this conversation. Emma flung another fistful of applesauce at Gabriel, mostly catching his left pajama-top lapel. Gabe barely noticed, intent on pursuing his line of inquiry.

"But, I mean, what did he *do*?" pressed Gabe.

"Well, I don't really know for sure, Gabe!" Mrs. McGregor was suddenly quite animated, and not too happy. She'd turned around, and was looking Gabe square in the eye. "He was a bean counter, for all I know!"

Emma caught the edge of a plastic spork that'd been dangling on the edge of her plate with her flailing hand, and launched it across the kitchen floor, along with the applesauce that it contained. She chirped in happiness, but both Gabriel and his mother took no notice.

"A bean what-er?" asked Gabe.

"A bean—Oh, I DON'T KNOW!" And in a fit, Susan McGregor flailed her arms above her head, then slapped a cloth she'd been holding *smack!* onto the counter. She mumbled something about needing to get dressed, and "not having time for this," and stormed out of the kitchen and up the stairs to her bedroom.

Gabriel was a little shocked by his mother's raw nerves on the subject, but not *too* surprised. He did get the distinct feeling as well, that she might be hiding something from him. All in good time though, he felt, and he decided to give his mom's behavior a good thinking-over later in the bath.

He looked over at Emma, who, an instant later, realized that all the food, and thus all the fun, was gone—and so was Mommy for that matter—so she began to wail, red-faced.

Cute little Emma. The slightly sour apple of Gabriel's eye. She was a silly little child Gabriel felt, although undeniably cute. She was only five years old and not nearly the grownup of eleven that was Gabriel, and although he loved his sister dearly, he felt that she would never, ever catch on, and was as much a nuisance than a ball of fun, which, to be fair, she definitely could be, given the right day.

So their school-less summer mornings would typically start like this: Emma would arise first, and it was then her self-appointed duty to slip into Gabriel's room and roust her groggy brother with a sharp poke to the ribcage—or whatever vulnerable, sensitive body part was laying exposed—which would invariably prompt Gabriel to dart out of bed and chase his little sister around the room, her hair bouncing and her giggles filling the air. Gabriel usually wasn't in a giggling mood when he lunged for his sister left and right, but this only made Emma laugh even harder. It was when Gabriel finally caught the pajama-clad Emma, her eyes gleaming, did Gabriel's mood lighten and laughs spill out of him too. Yep, he loved his sister, even if she was a pain on occasion.

Suitably awake, the pair would then follow the sumptuous waft of pancakes on the griddle, butter melting, and syrup pouring, right down the stairs and straight into the kitchen. There, their un-showered and tussle-haired mother would beam her unconditional love toward her two children, as best she could through her worried demeanor, hungry as they were. *That's the best part about having kids*, she would think. *Feeding them.*

Alight in their chairs, Gabriel would begin the proceedings by grabbing this, and Emma would reply by snatching that, and the next thing you knew, the pancakes were toast.

"Calm down, guys," Mom would intone, if her mood was light. "There's no rush. You have all day!"

Fair enough, Gabriel thought, but a day off from school is to be savored by cramming as much into it as possible. And indeed, only moments later, the pancakes already a distant memory, it would be time to officially start scheming. And after the previous evening's momentous events in the basement, Gabriel had plenty of scheming to do today. Those previous night's momentous events had transpired thusly.

The *clack* of the seventh lock felt good. It was dark and quiet in the kitchen, and well past midnight, but

Gabriel knew he had to make sure that his mother was dead asleep before he attempted any of his forays into the basement.

His homemade lock-picking device hadn't failed him yet, and he gave himself a good pat on the back for being clever. He then slowly and quietly pulled the door shut behind him, and at the top of the stairs, clicked on the light.

A bluish hue emanated from below, and Gabriel made his way carefully down the steps. Even though he'd done this many times in the past—since he was seven years old, if he had to guess—he still felt a thrill of excitement when he made the landing at the bottom of the stairs, and beheld the room that was the anteroom to his father's sanctuary.

At first glance, it wasn't anything special. Nothing more than a waiting room, it seemed. A sofa, two plush chairs, a coffee table, some side tables and lamps filled the space, with a doorway to the right that lead to a bathroom, and a doorway straight ahead that lead to the good stuff. The buzzing blue overhead lights gave the waiting room a moody twist—one that was welcome late at night.

Gabriel always stopped and admired the art that hung on the walls, most likely also admired in the past by his father's co-patriots, as they sat in this very room, waiting for him to emerge from his chamber of secrets. Large abstract pieces that weren't prints. Real art. Was his father an art collector too? He knew so little about his father, it angered him.

Gabriel stepped forward and opened the door that lead to the laboratory. Before him was a short, dark hallway, that was suddenly brightened by buzzing, blue overhead lamps, with Gabriel's flick of a switch. More art on each wall, then at the end of the hall, a right-hand turn into a large, almost cavernous room, echoing with dark dampness. Another flick of a switch, and more bluish light filled the space. Gabriel beheld the lab before him and, as each time before, felt admiration mixed with fear, topped off with an electric excitement. He knew to the bottom of his heart that something extremely important lived here, but he had absolutely no idea what it was.

He'd spent many hours in this very space trying to figure it out, however. And he had resources at his command. To his right, the entire wall was a bookshelf. It once held a book in every available space. Gabriel had determined by scratch marks on the shelves that many of the books had been quickly taken, but half of them were still there. To his left was what remained of a bank of computers: Many monitors and CPUs, but nearly all had had their hard drives removed. There was only one functioning computer left, as far as Gabriel could tell, and that one was locked down by a password.

It didn't take long for Gabriel to conclude that his father's lab had been pilfered, and that quickly, most likely the day he died. This tweaked Gabriel's curiosity, making him think that his father's death was a complicated affair. But as of yet, he had no idea what exactly was taken, or why.

A few feet further down on the left-hand wall sat the workbench, which was Gabriel's favorite spot. Aside from all the standard tools one might find on a workbench, there also sat a handful of very strange, inexplicable machines, or probably rather the skeletal remains thereof. Once again, it seemed to Gabriel, that things had been taken. Or possibly the machines were never completed. It was impossible to say which.

But the real curiosity was the large, forbidding wall that faced Gabriel from the farthest end of the chamber. It was a stone wall, but it was clear that someone tried to break through it at one time, in a rather violent fashion. There were many deep gouge marks many feet long, and chunks of rock on the floor below. Gabriel always got a chill when he saw this, and he'd come to the conclusion that whatever truth he might be looking for in regard to his father, sat directly behind that wall. Far be it for him to think that he'd have better luck getting through it than whoever had first shot at it, so he did what he always did, and ambled back over to the library shelves and picked up a favorite book of his—*Elementary Particle Physics in the Quantum Realm*. He leafed through it, pretending to know what he was looking at. Mostly, he liked the cool diagrams.

As he flipped through the pages, he sat down and booted up the sole working computer, wanting to have another go at guessing the password.

Once booted, the computer sported its very plain interface—black, with a white rectangle in the center, with the word Logon and a blinking cursor inside, asking to be filled in with letters and numbers.

Gabriel had only one shot at guessing the password each time he came down to visit. Whoever designed the system set it up so that a wrong password shut the computer down for at least twenty-four hours.

As Gabriel leafed through the book, admiring the highly detailed schematics of supercolliders and the like, he absentmindedly typed his mother's maiden name—Griffin—backwards, into the password field, and plunked down the Enter key. Expecting the boink and hum of shutdown that he'd become accustomed to, he kept flipping through the book, drawn to the increasingly interesting drawings.

It took him a good fifteen seconds to realize that he hadn't heard the boink of failure, nor the spin down of powered down hard drives.

He looked up in confusion, only to see a list of data streaming down the screen like a waterfall. His heart leaped. He was in! A moment later, the scrolling data stopped, and something resembling a desktop appeared on the screen. Gabriel held his breath. He slowly breathed out, and satisfied he wasn't imagining things. He grabbed the mouse and was an instant away from clicking a strange icon that drew his attention, when he heard some thumps above his head.

All went dead silent in Gabriel's mind, except for the pounding of blood through his veins and the primal fear welling up from his feet, chilling him as it went. If he was caught down here, he'd be in more trouble than he could imagine, and he'd never be able to figure out his father's secrets. His mother would destroy it all, he was sure.

A few torturous seconds ticked by, then Gabriel heard the sound he was dreading most: the metallic clack of the basement doorknob turning.

As if electrocuted, Gabriel shot into action, shutting down the computer, and bolting from his chair. He ran out of the lab, shutting off the light as he went, then hurtled himself down the short interconnecting hallway. He swung open the door leading into the anteroom and was rearing up to leap forward like a jaguar, when he was stopped mid-lunge by the visage of his little sister in her jammies, looking up at him like she'd just seen Santa Claus.

Gabriel's heart fluttered and his dread morphed to glee, then to anger in an instant.

"Emma!" Gabriel yelled.

"Whaaaaaa!" was Emma's shocked, bawling response.

"Quiet, quiet!" Gabriel intoned under his breath, grabbing his sister by the shoulder and pulling her toward him. She obeyed, but there was fear in her large blue eyes.

"What are you doing down here? You're supposed to be in bed, fer gosh sakes!"

"I dunno," Emma croaked. "I were thirsty, so I came down heres." She quietly sobbed a bit for emphasis.

Gabriel's eyes darted from side to side. "Okay," he said. "No harm done. Let's go up, and I'll put you back to bed." He stood up and took her by the hand. He took a step toward the stairs but felt resistance. He looked down at Emma and saw the back of her head, her feet planted, taking in the basement and hallway with full curiosity.

"What is here?" she asked.

"Emma! Let's go!"

"What is here?" she insisted.

"I'll tell you later. Now let's go, before Mom finds out!"

"No!" Emma spat, lower jaw jut forward. "I wanna see!"

"Emma!"

"Whaaaaaa!"

"Emma, stop!"

"Whaaaaa!" Emma hollered, exponentially gaining volume.

"Okay, okay!" beseeched Gabriel. "I'll show you!"

"Okay," Emma replied, smiling, without the slightest tinge of cry left in her tone.

From the outside, the McGregor's house was quite normal. It was a single family, three-story, two-car-garage home sitting unblinking beside its neighbors, in a moribund suburban landscape, with nothing seemingly out of kilter. But for an unusually large number of antennas that protruded from the roofline and the strange brass front-door knocker that always fascinated Gabriel, even before he could reach it, everything about this house and where it sat was mind-numbingly average.

In fact, everything about the McGregor's themselves was—until a few years ago, anyway—mind-numbingly average. The suburban, middle-American average. The keep up with the Jones average. The husband with a nine to five government job, the wife keeping house and raising two kids average. The mow your lawn every Sunday like everybody else, lest tempt your neighbors ire about their declining real estate values be tweaked, average. Everything average. That is, until Gabriel's dad died.

At least he had sympathy for his mother's hatred of this floor of the house, but Gabriel was determined to learn as much about his father as possible, and his mother wasn't telling him squat. He felt it more than fair that he should break her stringent rules. It was, he concluded, his duty, as his father's son, so he could properly uphold his father's legacy. Mom just didn't get that, yet.

So, it was with this sentiment sifting through his thoughts, that he realized it was only fair that Emma knew a thing or two about her father, as well, and he calmed himself to the point of brotherly caring, as he walked her through their father's hidden lair for the first time.

Hand-in-hand, they walked back through the connecting hallway, toward the lab. Emma's eyes were rolling this way and that, trying to take everything in. Although he figured he was imagining it, Gabriel felt that Emma was growing up a bit before his eyes. There was a subtle fierceness in her stare that told him that, young as she was, she understood that something very meaningful for her was down here.

She was so fascinated by what she was seeing that she barely made a peep. Maybe she was worried that

Gabriel would tell her to be quiet again, but Gabriel sensed that something else was going on. Her small child brain seemed to be computing as hard and as fast as it could, with every new detail that she took in. All she could manage was a couple of "What's dat?" She didn't even wait for a reply. She simply moved on to the next strange detail of this new environment, seemingly in a trance.

Gabriel smirked at the computer that he'd finally hacked into but was forced to shut down in panic, and stewed in an unquenchable desire to reboot it. He knew it was fruitless for tonight though, and it made him sad. He'd be forced to wait one more day, so wait he would. What he didn't realize though was that while he was salving his emotional wounds, he'd let go of Emma's hand, and she took the opportunity to reach toward the work bench and grab one of the small, strange devices that her brilliant father had left behind. It fit nicely in her hand, was roundish, had cute, happy colors on it, some eye-like glass, and metal bits, and it began to glow at her touch. She made a happy cat-like squeak and quickly stuffed it into the pouch of her jammies, knowing instinctively as a bird knows to yank a worm out of the ground, that is was hers, and only hers. Gabriel turned to take her hand, did, and was none the wiser about Emma's new toy. Before he knew it, the two of them were back upstairs in the kitchen, and Gabriel was locking the last of the seven locks on the basement door. He looked down at Emma with a seriousness about him, as slits of moonlight cut across the two of them.

"You can't tell Mom that we were down there, right?"

"Okay," she agreed; almost too agreeable, it seemed to Gabriel. He pressed on.

"You can't tell Mom about any of this, ever, as long as you live. You understand?"

Emma's eyes widened a bit, as if she was grasping the sleeve of some inexplicable enormity. "Okay," she said.

"And this is really important, Emma. I'm the only one allowed down there, ever again. It's my place and my place o—"

"No!" Emma blurted, suddenly out of her agreeable reverie; a hurt look on her cute little face.

"I wanna go! I wanna g—"

Gabriel panicked, putting a hand over Emma's mouth, so only muffled sounds made their way through his fingers. Her bright blue eyes were wide with shock, and implored up at Gabriel with fear, hurt, and betrayal. Gabriel caved in at once, understanding immediately that not only did Emma deserve to know about her father as much as he did, but also if he didn't include her in his explorations, she'd suss him out to their mother in no time flat.

"Okay! Okay!" he whispered to her loudly and empathically. Her eyes calmed a bit, and he released his hand from her mouth. Gabriel's eyes twitched nervously from side to side. He leaned in toward Emma.

"Shhhh," he implored softly, with his left forefinger to his lips. The only sound was the two of them breathing. Once Gabriel was convinced that his mother had not been awakened, he took Emma by the hand, and they walked quietly through the kitchen, and up the stairs. His thoughts were a fear-inspired jumble of what-ifs, understanding that Emma's involvement added a level of complexity and unpredictability to this whole affair that was daunting, to say the least. When they reached the top landing of the stairs, however, he calmed himself with the insight that what Emma didn't know wouldn't hurt her, and he had the only lock-picking device, anyway, so he could come and go as he pleased, and only invite Emma along if she became a pain about it. He could even make up stories about discovering monsters down there, he surmised, patting himself on the back for being clever. That would keep her away from the basement for a few years, he would bet.

After tucking Emma back into bed and making his way to his bedroom, his brain started filling with the excitement of the next evening. He almost never tempted fate by going down to the basement two nights in a row, but he had to, this time. He'd discovered the password! He was in! He was so overwhelmed with fantasies about what he might find, that he laid in bed for hours, eyes closed, seeing all the possibilities in his mind's eye. He didn't know it, but he eventually fell asleep with a satisfied grin on his face. It kept until morning.

The next morning—this morning—after Susan McGregor's odd emotional display, and after Gabe and Emma had retreated to their rooms, Emma burst into Gabriel's room just as he was putting the finishing touches on donning his daily wardrobe—pulling up his left sock, to be precise.

"Gabriel! Look at my new thing!" she squealed gleefully. She was holding the device she'd found the night previous as if presenting it as a gift.

Gabriel was suitably peeved by Emma's sudden interruption.

"You're supposed to knock! Mom says you're supposed to knock!"

Emma felt a tad admonished and pulled the device to her chest. "But it's got warm eyes"—her finger pointing things out—"and a blue antenna, and it shows movies in my head, and a green and yellow…"

"It's just a toy, Emma! Big deal. I don't have time for this kid's stuff." Gabriel stood up as if to underscore his point, not realizing that he'd totally missed the bigger point. It looked like just another one of Emma's silly toys to Gabe. "I've got many important things to do today. I'll look at it later. Maybe." He then marched past his sister and out of his room, feeling as important as he knew he was. Emma stood there and watched him leave, feeling silly to her core. She felt embarrassed that she was still wearing her pajamas, and her big brother was dressed and doing important things already. She shuffled back to her room, inspecting her new, strange, other-worldly toy, but feeling sort of guilty and sad about the whole thing, and not knowing why.

Meanwhile, Gabriel was preparing for the big day ahead by thinking. Gabriel did this often. It was what separated him from most other humans, he felt. The fact that he actually used his brain as much as possible instead of feeding it with silly television shows and badly designed video games until it swelled with the empty fats of disuse and atrophy, made him most proud of himself. But he wasn't beyond television or video games on occasion, as he was just a kid after all. And in fact, his first line of reasoning of the morning concluded with the conclusion that his first important act of the day was to watch a few minutes of his favorite cartoons, in order to clear his mental palate for what lie ahead. It was there, situated most comfortably in front of the tube, absorbing the existential angst of his favorite cartoon, *Mack the Machine-Man*, that Emma came skipping into the living room, trumpeting her new device as before. At least, Gabriel noticed, she'd had the decency to put on proper clothing.

"Gabriel! Look! It plays a space song!" Emma squealed happily. Her timing couldn't have been worse, as Mack had just launched into one of his beautifully angry rants, the likes of which entertained Gabriel quite a bit.

"I know, Emma! Leave me alone! I'll look at it later!" he fussed.

This time Emma was too angry to be hurt. She jut out her lower lip, her face turned red as a beet, and she turned on a dime and stormed out of the living room. Gabriel steamed under his collar too because he'd just missed a piece of cartoon magic, all because of his well-meaning but very silly, silly sister.

Taking this encounter as a cue to move onto his next important task, Gabriel decided to do some learning and stuck his face into the thick and oddly pleasant-smelling pages of his late father's Physics book—the one that made it possible for him to embarrass his classmates and at times even his teacher with scientific knowledge beyond his years.

Plus, Gabriel's dad had passed away when he was just a baby, and these books were a way for him to get to know his father just a little bit.

"Let's see," Gabriel mused as he flipped through large, ink-filled pages. "How about Inertia and Momentum today? Maybe I'll be able to show that stupid-head Kurt why his batting technique sucks." His mission properly laid out, Gabriel set about reading and comprehending the lengthy text with full satisfaction. But not a half an hour later, he was fast asleep, using the book as an inadvertent pillow. He began to dream:

A bright, lovely day. Gabriel was in an unknown town that nonetheless seemed familiar. He walked shop-lined streets and was very curious about what was around each corner, yet, with each turn onto another unknown street, he felt a sense of loneliness that intensified the more he explored.

He followed streets that curved up steep hills then down again, always hoping to find a place he was familiar with just past the next group of buildings, but never succeeding.

The sun began to set, and Gabriel set foot onto a dirty and rundown street that scared him. He turned around to backtrack to safer ground, but realized that he was suddenly in the middle of a very bad neighborhood, without any idea of how he'd gotten there.

People of suspicious nature eyed him from across streets, making Gabriel feel extremely vulnerable. He began looking for hiding places between buildings, and running through yards and parking lots to make quick pass into other neighborhoods. But it kept getting darker and darker, and Gabriel became more and more desperate for sanctuary.

It was then that Gabriel became aware of an ominous presence that was stalking him. It might have been neighborhood punks, he conceded to himself, but it seemed to be something a bit more treacherous, even evil.

Gabriel ran as hard as he could. He slid down backyards and slipped between fences, all the while quite convinced that the entity that was chasing him was only moments away from catching and killing him. And it was at the absolute moment of truth when all seemed lost, and the monster's breath could be felt on his neck, did Gabriel remember that he could fly! And instantly as if on cue, he left the ground and flung up into the sky, light as a kite and in total control of his soaring flight.

He surveyed the ground beneath him, taken aback by the beauty of it all, and by his newfound sense of absolute freedom and total safety. This was his natural state, he thought to himself—to be alone with his thoughts and free to go wherever he wished, at the moment he wished it!

Suddenly, unhappily, he was back on the ground, it was daylight again, and he was standing next to Emma, but she was taller than he and very serious about everything. No fun aloud. She said, "Look at this." And then handed him a picture of an odd, disfigured person. "Wait here a moment," she added, and walked off with an air of indifference. Gabriel was scared at being left alone, so he began searching for Emma, but couldn't find her anywhere.

He was turning a corner onto a bleak, empty street, when suddenly like an explosion, Emma's angry, now-demonic face filled his full vision and screeched, "NEVER!"

Gabriel awoke in a hot sweat, book pages stuck to his sticky face. He righted himself as best he could, then gave himself a moment to wake up and absorb the dream he'd just had. He concluded that it didn't mean much and was simply a collection of odd images and feelings spit out randomly by his sleeping brain. But it did haunt him for a while, even as he sat in front of the television playing his favorite shoot-'em-up video game. Actually, he was unable to enjoy it as he had hoped, as the dream continually ran through his head.

It's time for a bath, he thought to himself. *Baths always makes me feel better.*

Gabriel sat back in the tub, and hot, bubble-bathed water washed over him. He wasn't the splash-about kind of kid when it came to taking a bath, although it was true he would indulge in such tomfoolery when the mood struck. But mostly Gabriel enjoyed the peace and quiet that a nice hot bath afforded him, because—once again—it gave him an excellent opportunity to think. In fact, it was the most ideal time to sort things out in his head, being in a bath. *There's something about water*, he'd think to himself.

Today, as he closed his eyes and began to mull over whatever his brain was on about, he couldn't help but feel a tinge of the dream he'd had earlier, fainter though it was. And it started him thinking about himself, for some reason, and how others might perceive him. He'd always felt quite confident that the world at large liked him, but somehow, deep down, he was beginning to feel glimmers of a doubt. *Does Emma hate me?* he thought. But then, *Why should I worry about her opinion about me, anyway? She's just a confused kid. Emma should love me… I'm a great kid! Everybody should love me.*

Gabriel was thinking a mile a minute now, but this time he wasn't enjoying it like he usually did. Too much self-doubt.

I'm a good kid, he reassured himself. *I do the dishes every other night, without a single complaint. That's gotta be worth something. I help Emma with her homework, like a good brother. I mow the lawn when my mom asks me too. Heck, I even enjoy it! Plus, I get good grades, and I rarely have a bad thought or word for anyone else, except maybe Emma, I guess. I suppose I could be a bit nicer to her. I'm a good kid, and that's all there is to it!*

Suitably reassured, Gabriel let out a sigh and put the matter out of his head for the moment. Happily, thoughts of the physics of Inertia and Momentum took its place.

Meanwhile, Emma was in her room—directly across the hall from the bathroom—and was as determined as ever to prove to Gabriel once and for all that her new thing was awesome! This time, she was going to have it spinning in midair as it showed her it could do, and speaking its own very odd language, before she even approached Gabriel, the more likely to impress him into realizing the true brilliance of the thing.

Gabriel was in a kind of nirvana, now. His troubled mind put to rest, his eyes were sleeping, and his mind wandering, conjuring up all kinds of mental oddities. His imagination slipped into a place where Emma had morphed into a three-faced dartboard, and he, himself, was a robot made from ice cream cones. He had nearly figured out how the dartboard met the robot (with the

help of a policefish?), when Emma burst into the bathroom, clutching her wonderful, new, toy-friend firmly
in both hands, as it emitted musical howls the likes of
a late-night horror film, glowed throbbingly in a rainbow, and actually seemed to grow in size.

Gabriel shot bolt-upright, having been ripped from
his reverie in a most inglorious fashion. Meanwhile,
Emma's stride hit a slippery bath mat, and her momentum pulled her forward as she slipped, like a skater hit-
ting wet ice. Having just read a very detailed chapter on
the physics of movement, Gabriel could predict quite
accurately what was only microseconds from transpiring. And, unfortunately for him, it transpired just so.
Emma, "skating" on the bathmat, slammed into the
edge of the bathtub just as the water that was displaced
by Gabriel's sudden lurch upward began to splash back
down. But before that happened, Gabriel made a gallant
attempt at saving the day by catching Emma's throbbing, moaning techno space ball as it shot forward from
her now very confused outstretched hands. However,
he couldn't fight the inexorable pull of gravity, and with
the thing hugged tightly to his chest, he slipped back
down into the water as it splashed back down into the
tub and all over Gabriel's now fatally electrocuted body.

ON TO THE AFTERLIFE

GABRIEL'S SHOCK AND pain and surprise melted into an infinite singularity of light and love, and surprisingly he felt no fear from the horror that'd just transpired. He realized that his body had died—at least, that's the explanation that made the most sense to him—but he was still very much alive, and as far as he could tell, he was still himself, just ethereal, not material.

And he seemed to be traveling—heading toward The Light. That show he'd seen on the Discovery Channel about near-death experiences was right! Like a tractor beam, this golden shaft of light drew Gabriel toward its welcoming source, emanating eternal love, and filling his heart with profound peace and joy. It didn't take a rocket scientist to figure this one out. Gabriel was going to Heaven!

So he relaxed and sped along, like riding a wave, waiting for the sublime moment when he was to enter Heaven.

A tug.

A downward tug on Gabriel's soul. It seemed innocuous at first, but worrisome all the same. He then felt another, as if someone was trying to pull him underwater—if he'd been swimming, for instance—but it only lasted a moment and was gone. Gabriel was still riding the light toward Heaven, but now sensed that he was in a race of extreme consequence.

Another tug. Stronger. Gabriel seemed to slow down a bit this time. But he regained his clip all the same. An even stronger tug, then, and Gabriel's momentum began to seriously wane, as if he'd entered molasses. *How dream-like*, Gabriel mused, and he began hoping above hope that this whole ridiculous affair was only a dream.

Like a locomotive revving its engine to get its giant weight moving, he slowly began to regain momentum, but it was hard. He soon felt something grasp his essence in its tight, tentacle-like grip, and this time, whatever held him was not about to let go. Gabriel's heart sank with despair. He knew to his core that his soul (which was actually all he was at the moment) was being kidnapped, and that something very bad was about to happen to him.

He was now stopped dead in his tracks, the entrance to Heaven happily shimmering tantalizingly close, but impossible to reach. The round, golden entryway then dimmed into a dark, rich red, and Gabriel's tormentor yanked him downward with vengeful force one last time, into complete darkness.

Gabriel was in a room. He was standing there, a physical boy again, in the middle of a bright, white room. It was about twenty foot square, he wagered, and it was entirely empty and void of all detail except for a black dot in the middle of one particular wall. He walked toward the dot and gave it a closer look. It was a button. It said Push on it.

Gabriel was not about to push this button, because he knew in his heart what would happen if he did, and he certainly didn't want *that* to happen! So he turned and walked across the room and sat down against the wall farthest from the button. And he watched the button suspiciously, and he began to think.

I'm in hell. I know I am. Or at least I'm on my way there, it would seem. No, I'm not dreaming, and this certainly isn't Heaven, so, yes, it has to be Hell, or someplace like Hell, such as Purgatory, possibly. Mom told me about Purgatory. But something tells me, if I push that button, I will go straight to Hell, regardless. Something deep inside tells me that, quite strongly.

Gabriel eyed the button with an empty countenance, having nothing more to think about. What else is there to think about when you're stuck in a box that's probably the last stop before Hell? Nothing. And Gabriel sat for what seemed like hours, not thinking at all. This was a first for him. Not a single real thought, except for the button. Then, oddly enough, he fell asleep:

Darkness, as one might expect. But just enough light— a brownish light—for Gabriel to see his body, as he lay jammed into the corner of what seemed to be a small, small room. He'd pulled himself together into a fetal position, with his legs and arms seemingly stick-like, as if carved from wood. As was fitting, he was frozen stiff by a comatose-like fear.

With pitch black beginning only inches from his extremities, the other side of this hellish little dwelling might as well have been a million miles away.

He began to sense very strongly that there were beings just beyond the veil of darkness, watching him, judging him, and testing him, as if he was nothing more than a wild animal, having been bagged for study. How incredibly vulnerable he felt, as if he were a babe in womb fearing the thrust of a surgeon's scalpel at any moment.

He closed his eyes, but that didn't help. How could it? When he reopened his eyes, however, what he beheld horrified him to his marrow!

His entire field of view was filled with a face—a metallic and menacing face—and it stared down at him with large, oval eyes that seemed to absorb Gabriel's very being. Instinctively, Gabriel tried to determine an entomology or genus of similar earth creatures, but he came up blank, since the face seemed human and insect at the same time, or rather something "other." Regardless, these musings gave his mind something to occupy itself for a few thankful moments, instead of dwelling upon a swift welling up of sheer terror from the pit of his belly, which was his only other option.

After a fashion, Gabriel was able to calm down slightly, because, strangely, the horrid façade made no sounds, nor moved its mouth—its eyes blinked only, and some facial muscles occasionally twitched.

A few more moments passed, and Gabriel actually became slightly comfortable, feeling more like he was watching a movie of some kind. The thought occurred to him that perhaps this thing that was engulfing his perception was actually a projection of sorts and not really here—none but a harmless specter.

"I AM NOT HARMLESS!" screeched the face, pining Gabriel's stick-like body to the wall with knives of terror.

"In fact, I'm the MASTER OF HARM! The DEFINITION OF FEAR! This, you will deeply understand, ALL TOO SOON!"

Gabriel tried to weasel away from the shrieking harpy by pushing his terrified body along the wall behind him, but the ghoulish head kept itself aligned perfectly in Gabriel's full vision, blocking his every attempt at escape. Gabriel gave up and slumped to the floor.

"I am METZORQ, keeper of the Box," he continued, "and servant to the Master. All who are sent below pass through me." Gabriel noticed a foul whiff flowing from Metzorq's mouth, this time.

"Now you will understand: there is no other reason for your existence in my house except to do the one thing that you, and everyone who's ever come here, must do and always has done throughout all of time." Gabriel knew exactly what Metzorq was going to say. "You must push the button!"

Yep, thought Gabriel. *I knew it.* Regardless, he tried to reason with the demon.

"I…I…can't push the button, I—"

"YOU MUST!" came the thunderous, evil wind.

"But then I'll go to hell," Gabriel blabbered, half-crying. "I don't want to go to—"

"HAH HAH HAHA HAAAH!" belly-laughed the beast. And belly-laughed continually, he did. And after a few minutes of this, Gabriel realized that Metzorq showed absolutely no sign of stopping this boisterous, almost jolly belly-laughing.

In fact, tears began to stream down Metzorq's cheeks, and his laughing became increasingly louder and more tickled as the moments passed, to the point where Gabriel was beginning to see the humor of the whole thing too.

Gabriel was nearly on the verge of exploding with side-splitting laughter himself—preferring to be in on the joke instead of the butt of it—when Metzorq's oddly inhuman visage began morphing into something more comprehensible and much more sinister. And as Gabriel considered this transformation, he realized that Metzorq's head had become that of a giant cricket's, featuring antenna, pincers, and everything else one would find on a cricket head, all moving and twisting to the beat of the laughing, which incidentally had begun to sound more like deep, mournful cries from the pit of a very disturbed soul, indeed.

And before Gabriel could fully comprehend this disturbing development, Metzorq the Cricket Head opened his insect mouth and lunged at Gabriel, grasping Gabriel's small, vulnerable head in his sickening, machine-like mandibles. Metzorq then, over the objection of Gabriel's jerking, twisting and screaming protests, began to crush him to pieces and slowly and with relish devour him, chewing Gabriel's matter slowly, down to its very molecular constituents, with Gabriel feeling every moment of every grind of Metzorq's insectoid jaws and teeth. All in all, it was quite painful.

Gabriel awoke with a start, his bloodshot eyes bulging from his red, sweaty head. He could still feel the pain from the cricket's unstoppable, machine-like jaw, cracking through his skull bones. He shuddered. *God, I hope that really was a dream*, he considered. *However, I am in hell, or at least I seem to be. Who knows what's real and what's not?* A reasonable supposition from a reasonable young man.

Gabriel looked across his prison at the button, and he was disturbed. It had grown in size. He didn't like that fact. It had gained the diameter of a baseball, it seemed, so Gabriel felt compelled to examine it again. He walked up to it and gave it the once over. Except for its increased size, all seemed normal.

Normal! Gabriel laughed to himself. *What an absurd concept!*

Still, the button—sporting Push on its flat surface as before—seemed no more sinister than any other button one might find. Gabriel felt it best not to even pretend to touch it, though. For all he knew, it had some sort of finger radar, and all he needed to do is stick his finger in close proximity, and *Bam!* Whatever bad thing that was slated to happen would indeed then happen. Gabriel thought it best to turn around and make for his end of the room, and that's precisely what he did. And after he settled into his space, he turned to look at the button, all the while considering what bizarre happenstance was only moments away from occurring, because, if Gabriel had learned anything in his small span of time visiting this place, it was that there were few moments of boring nothingness. How he longed for boring nothingness, right now. The first time in his life he'd ever felt that way, Gabriel wagered.

He was tired, and he rubbed his eyes. When he opened them, he couldn't help but notice that the button had grown again, and not unsubstantially. In fact, it was more than twice its previous size, with a diameter befitting a basketball. Gabriel was flummoxed for a moment, but he wasn't stupid. He guessed what was in store. He closed, then opened his eyes again, and sure enough, the button had doubled in size once more, forcing Gabriel to deduce the ignominy to come, because the button was now large enough that it seemed to be reaching out for Gabriel, and after doing a little quick math, he surmised that he had but three more opportunities to close his eyes until the button, seemingly smiling at him at this very moment (Gabriel knew not how), would actually crush poor Gabriel's ethereal but frail body.

Gabriel thought about what it might mean to be crushed in hell. Not actually being alive and solid—but apparently being just that, if looks were to be believed—Gabriel figured that being crushed was an impossibility. Of course, it also occurred to Gabriel that hell is all about the art of suffering, so he figured, if not actually crushed, he sure would feel the unpleasantness of it all right. Good enough reason to try his best to avoid the crushing, if in fact he could. *Best keep my eyes open at all cost*, he said to himself. *Could be a problem achieving that though, although I did read once about a man who'd taught himself how to sleep with his eyes open. Wonder if I could do that now?* Gabriel sighed deep and heavy in thought of his predicament. *Man*, he pondered. *Hell really sucks!*

Gabriel had again fallen asleep. As unlikely as it may seem to actually need sleep while existing in another non-mortal dimension, the fact was, after a fashion—

just as it was when he was alive on earth—he felt dog tired and was forced to lay down, close his lids, and commence what seemed to be, for all intents and purposes, the act of sleeping.

This time around, Gabriel had been granted a reprieve, apparently, because during this particular snore, there were no giant cricket heads chasing him around and grinding him to dust in their massive, phlegmy jaws. No, this time, he dreamt only of a single daisy. It was tall and proud and swayed ever so slightly in the breeze. The day was profoundly beautiful: the hills carpeted with gorgeous, green grass, and the sky a placid blue filled with billowy white clouds.

The entire dream consisted of this daisy and nothing else. For what seemed like hours. Just the daisy. Gabriel couldn't change his point of view, and he'd tried. But all he could see was the daisy. That stupid daisy!

Anyway, as is inevitable in situations such as these, Gabriel eventually woke up. And while for a brief moment he could think of nothing but daisies, when he turned his head, he thought of nothing but the button. That stupid button! It was now only a few feet from his face, completely filling his entire little room like a beach ball stuffed into a lunch box. Gabriel even began to believe that he'd run out of air and was suffocating. And like most people would in situations like this, he rubbed his confused and haggard face, the consequence being that he'd closed his eyes for just a moment. But the damage was done.

He was now being squeezed impossibly small into his sharp angular corner, feeling as if a mouse caught in a trash compactor. The discomfort was unbearable. He kept his eyes open as much as was possible, then turned his head millimeter by millimeter to face the button. It took a Herculean effort.

He could see the lower left hand serif of the letter *P*, shoved right into his face. He began to gasp for air. Using all of his strength and against the crushing pressure of the button, he pulled his right arm up toward his face, in an effort to create an air pocket for his smushed nose.

Gabriel simply couldn't take it anymore. With his right hand, palm turned out—not wanting to feel even one more second of the stifling crush—he pushed at the button. In other words, he pushed the button. And he was gone.

DEEPER INTO HADES

GABRIEL WAS FLOATING downward. And for the first time in his unexpected journey, he considered the fact that he was not deserving of his present fate. *Why am I in hell?* He questioned. *I definitely, positively do not deserve to be here! Unless, of course, what I was taught in Sunday school was just plain wrong. I have a hard time believing that though. No. I definitely do not deserve to be here!* Gabriel was becoming indignant, and rightfully so. But before he could wallow for long in his newfound sense of injustice, the darkness that had fallen around him since he pushed the big, inflated button began to give way to an ominous red light, and the further he floated downward, the brighter it became.

And the brighter it became, the more he could see, and Gabriel gasped to himself when he realized that all around him were souls just like his—most solemn faced—floating downward like a massive, rushing river of human discontent. And when he looked down, he realized that they were all headed into an unspeakably large cavern, the bottom of which glowed a ghastly bright red. *Oh my God! I really am going to hell!* It dawned on Gabriel, and he began to cry. And after whipping away some tears, he looked about to see others bursting into tears. He'd have hoped that his misery would love their company, but in this place, Gabriel realized, they just added to his misery.

And boy, was there ever misery! The closer Gabriel got to the bottom of the cavern, the more the suffering around him became less an idea and more a physical thing that had a life of its own—like a big, fat vat filled with tragic jello that soaked through every pore of Gabriel's being. He was literally drowning in sorrow.

And then, like a feather landing, Gabriel's feet touched ground—as did thousands around him—and he found himself on a gigantic ramp that angled down toward the source of the evil, red light. Something about setting his feet on the ground enabled him to settle himself emotionally to a degree, and as a result, he was able to look around and absorb his surroundings.

He looked up. *Classic hell*, Gabriel thought, as he spied the roof of the gigantic cavern he was dejectedly traversing. Millions of stalactites hung down, some as small as he, others seemingly the size of skyscrapers. *That's basically New York City in stone, hanging over my head*, he observed. And indeed it was, because what Gabriel couldn't detect because of the large distance and poor lighting were the hellish, demonic denizens of the cavern who lived upside-down in and around the roof rocks. Just as well he didn't know.

Being one, if not the only, child-soul that was on the ramp that day, all around him, packing him tight, were the knees and rumps of adult human souls who were damned along with Gabriel. So it was hard to see these people and get a sense of who they were and why they were here, but against his better judgment, Gabriel's curiosity took over as he grabbed the arm of a man next to him.

"WHYYYY?" screamed the man as he bent down and locked eyes with Gabriel's, although "eyes" is a loose description, because his seemed to be nothing but black, empty holes that let light into his skull cavity.

"WHHHYYYYYY?" He moaned again, grabbing Gabriel by the shoulders and shaking him fiercely. His jawbone slipped loose and hung like a ghost's. Gabriel instinctively wriggled out of the man's clutches and bounced between the thighs and knee bones of other souls in escape, until he felt marginally safe. He heard a woman's voice and looked up.

Gabriel beheld a youngish woman, whose momentary torture seemed to have been interrupted by Gabriel's appearance. She cried tears of happiness about which Gabriel had no understanding, then as she reached to grab him, he suddenly got the sense that these were genuinely bad people—in the throes of deep regret—and were reacting to Gabriel's pure, unsullied innocence, and were instinctively drawn to him as a possible way out of their deep, torturous pain. At least, that's what was occurring to Gabriel as this twisted, horrible woman hugged him tight around his rib cage and began crushing him, not out of enthusiasm, but seemingly to squeeze out just a drop of his innocent goodness. Gabriel stomped hard on her foot, she screamed in pain, and he popped out of her grip like a sprung trap. She murderously swiped at his small blond head as he disappeared into the crowd.

Gabriel bounced among legs and arms as he ran, more scared than he'd ever been. People—things, beings, eternally damned souls—grabbed at him, lunged at him, all attracted by his childlike spirit. He was creating a commotion, as if there weren't reason enough for commotion in hell anyhow.

He thudded into a man whose naked body was charred black and whose left arm was missing. "HEY!" the burned man shouted. "Be my friend! Please?" Gabriel had darted away too quickly to hear his pitiful request amongst the savage, thick din of moans, groans, and screams that reverberated through the cavern.

A moments more of running for his soul, and Gabriel ran smack dab into a large dog's posterior. The dog was drenched in blood that splashed Gabriel's fine attire red. The beast snapped around and lunged at Gabriel, growling the growl of the tormented. Gabriel was fast, but not fast enough, and the beast's jaw clenched down into the flesh of Gabriel's right forearm.

The pain stung like a dentist's drill to the bone, and Gabriel fell to his knees. Fortunately for him though, the dog had an owner and was leashed, and a moment later, the evil beast had released Gabriel and was healed at the feet of his master.

The injury to his arm was throbbing, and his blood was pumping out of the gash precipitously, and even though all of his feelings and instincts pointed to imminent death due to bloodletting, it struck him that he was already dead, and that he couldn't possibly die again. In fact, if he could, he'd want to, in order to get out of this place. But he knew he couldn't, because then it wouldn't be hell, would it?

"Hello, young man," came the soothing voice. It belonged to a gentleman of means seemingly, as he was dressed the way of the gentrified rich: nicely tailored three-piece suite, fashionably cut and styled hair, with an air of invincibility about him. Gabriel immediately felt safe, and the chaos that surrounded him seemed to melt into silence.

"You're quite the smart one," he commented. "It takes most souls a much longer period of time to come to the same conclusion. You're going to be a tough one, I can see."

Gabriel stared up at him vacantly.

"What a day you're having, huh?" he continued. "But I'm sure that you're not too surprised, considering where you are"

Gabriel was too overwhelmed to reply. He simply looked up at the man, and over at the dog—who incidentally was licking his fur quite happily, as if nothing of note had just transpired—and back at the man again, and back and forth, as the new stranger spoke.

"Stand up, young man. We have places to go."

Gabriel hesitated for a moment, but then regained enough fortitude to regain his feet. His arm had seemingly healed by itself in only moments. He made a mental note of that.

His surroundings had changed remarkably. He was alone with this man and his dog, and they were in a quiet place of infinite, yellow horizon. Everywhere he looked, he saw a yellowish-orange hue that seemed to stretch for miles and miles, and yet, the horizon was too distant seemingly to even see. It was as if there was nothing, anywhere, he concluded.

"Who are you?" Gabriel finally croaked as they walked, he knew not to where.

"I'm not who you probably think I am. I'm often confused for the big guy." He was grinning ear to ear.

Gabriel's heart skipped a beat. For an instant, he felt that maybe, just maybe, he'd been rescued from hell by an angel.

"Oh no!" said the man, reading Gabriel's thoughts. "I'm your personal tormentor! Everybody gets one. It's my job to carry out Satan's sentence on the damned. And that includes you, my young friend!"

Gabriel fell to his knees again, this time from the pain of shock. The tormentor's dog began to growl a low, rumbly growl, making clear his displeasure.

"Don't make Mabel mad, Gabriel, or you will regret it, I assure you." His tone had turned menacing and any sense of safety that Gabriel had felt only moments ago had twisted 180 degrees into crippling insecurity.

Gabriel responded to the threat by making an effort—however half-hearted—to arise from the ground. Impatient, Gabriel's tormentor's furrowed a brow, and Gabriel began to float upward. Before he knew it, he was looking down on the man and his dog, his limbs hanging limply at his side.

"Much better," said the man. Mabel barked a happy bark. Gabriel grimaced.

"Let's go," he continued, and as he walked, his bizarre dog at his side, Gabriel floated along with them, unable to do anything but float. He was quite helpless.

They walked for what seemed to be hours in total silence, except for the footfalls, of course. Mabel and her owner didn't even grant Gabriel the respect of looking his way even once, for they knew that he was tethered to them in a fashion that was unbreakable, so he was forgettable. He was like a bumper on a car. Tagging along without consent nor regard.

And as they walked, their surroundings changed not at all. It was almost as if they were on a treadmill, because the horizon—or what seemed to be the horizon—never seemed to get any closer. But Gabriel's captors were determined to get somewhere. There was no doubt in Gabriel's mind about that.

"By the way," the demonic gentlemen said, finally looking in Gabriel's direction, "my name is Paynelion."

"Pa—what?" came Gabriel's bemused reply.

"Paynelion!" the man exhorted. "Or Payne, for short. My name is legend in these parts, and souls hell-wide will be awed by the fact that I'm your tormentor! I deserve and demand your ultimate respect!"

Gabriel suddenly felt argumentative, and expressed his disdain to Payne: "I don't care what your name is! You're a jerk!"

Payne stopped short. Mabel did the same and looked up at Gabriel, an angry glint in her eyes. Gabriel hung in midair and felt like a piñata about to be busted open by the angry swing of a stick.

Payne stared at Gabriel for an eternity, then began to display symptoms of boiling anger: his hair cracked loose from its gel and jut out in all directions as if shocked by electricity. His face grew red at the same time that the veins in his neck swelled to a grotesque proportion. His shoulders hunched and his arms flexed like an ape, and Gabriel noticed that Mabel had stepped away, her tail between her legs. She was scared. Gabriel knew he was in for it now.

Sure enough, after what sounded like the short burst of a high-pitched squeal, Payne's body exploded into a giant red ball, almost balloon-like, and biological matter of all sorts of disgusting variety flung in all directions, including onto Gabriel's shocked face.

When Gabriel whipped the smelly detritus from his eyes, he beheld a large, angry, and round entity that oozed hurt, pain, maliciousness, and a deep red color that shone like an energy field. Payne's face covered the entire ball like a ghostly visage. It spoke:

"Here, where you are and always will be," he began with a tightly controlled quiver. "Names are very important indeed."

Gabriel was riveted.

"And you will learn the names of everyone that you meet, and you will utter them with the utmost respect, *if* you're called upon to utter them at all. You will never"—his pitch suddenly shot up—"and I mean, NEVER, be allowed to disrespect the names of your tormentors." He quieted down a bit. "This is your only warning. Believe me, you shan't wish to disobey this edict."

Gabriel gulped.

Payne, the big red ball, disappeared in a flash and was replaced with his previous well-mannered and manicured form.

"Okay!" he said with a skip in his voice. "Let's go!"

Mabel had been happily chewing a piece of meat that was previously a part of Payne, but she jerked to attention when he said *go*, dropped the slimy sinew from her maw, and the three of them began moving again. But before Gabriel could let out a full sigh, Payne and Mabel abruptly stopped and turned to him.

"Actually," Payne intoned, "I think we should begin our little sideshow with our new friend, right here and now! What do you think, Mabel?"

Mabel began to bark that happy bark that dogs bark when they're happy, her tail wagging spasmodically. And the faster her tail wagged, the hotter the pool of dread that suddenly appeared in the pit of Gabriel's belly burned. In fact, this particular feeling quite reminded him of a few rare instances in school when he'd be a bit too happy with himself, living inside his own little world and then, out of the blue, his teacher would call on him to answer a question for which he had no answer. A scary, shocking turn of events! Well, this was that too, only much, much, much more upsetting. Gabriel gulped the biggest gulp he'd ever gulped, then waited.

Payne and Mabel stared deep into Gabriel's eyes, and he began to feel queasy. And the more they stared, the more Gabriel felt compelled to stare back, being pulled into their dark soul chambers. Soon, all he could see was their menace—all else had faded to nothingness—and then, a moment later, he was blissfully asleep at home, and dreaming the best dream he'd ever dreamt. It had something to do with cheesecake and racecars, and that cute little blonde-haired girl in home room. She really liked him!

A poke. Gabriel tossed in his bed. Another poke, this one much harder.

"Ouch!" Gabriel screamed, being pulled from his reverie by the prod of Emma's index finger. He hated that feeling more than anything—being forcibly awakened from a transcendent dream—and he bolted upright to teach Emma a lesson. He lunged for her, but her muscles were awake and quicker, and she was impossible to catch.

"Aaaaggh!!! Stop it, Emma! I told you never to do that again!"

Emma laughed and laughed, and the few times Gabriel nearly tackled her, she slipped from his grip as if oiled like a pig. Her laughing irked his very soul and engendered his discontent to the point of extreme anger, which was unlike him, since he loved Emma very much. But this time she'd gone too far, Gabriel wagered, and he was very, very mad at her!

He was asleep again.

He was having the best dream he'd ever had.

A poke, and the cycle repeated itself. And if I had to guess, it repeated itself many thousands of times, each time Gabriel becoming slightly more aware of what was actually happening to him. And as his anger at Emma grew to impossible proportions—to the point where he actually wanted to kill her—his realization that he must not be back at home began to fill his consciousness, and it was at this point, at this realization, as Emma had slipped from his clutches once again, that Payne appeared to him. Gabriel knew it was Payne, even though it certainly looked nothing like him.

"You are a hard nut to crack, aren't you, Gabriel?"

Payne now looked more like a hairless chimpanzee, but with a large, melon-like head that vaguely resembled a dinosaur's. Gabriel figured it most like a brachiosaurus's.

They were still in Gabriel's bedroom, but Emma was gone. Gabriel was in his pajamas, and Payne—in this form—smelled like a crate filled with rotting sea creatures. Gabriel flinched and his nose flared.

"Yes, indeed. You figured that one out quickly, didn't you? It often takes most souls a few centuries of torture to realize their predicament. You, however, realized after only a couple of months. Impressive! You're a challenge, my young friend! How exciting! You'll get my A-game, that's for sure, because I have a reputation of the highest order to uphold down here."

Gabriel didn't quite know how to take this news. Certainly he was flattered, even given the bizarre circumstances, and yet, it also meant that he was in for a more severe degree of torment than was originally planned.

"Relax!" Payne reassured. "Everybody here is tormented for eternity. I'll just have to be a bit more clever about you."

"Great," muttered Gabriel.

WE'RE OFF TO SEE THE DEVIL

"I DON'T BELONG here!" Gabriel shrieked at his tormentor as Payne tickled the bottom of his left foot. He'd been doing this for over fifty hours. Tickling can be fun, I suppose, but fifty hours of nonstop ticking is quite unbearable indeed. And here in hell, it's impossible to get used to something or tune it out. Each tickle is as intense as the first, and it simply never stops.

This ragtag ensemble of three had returned to the empty place of yellowness where they'd begun their journey together. Gabriel was floating in the air, and Payne stood below him—the better to get a proper angle—flicking a feather at his bare feet. Mabel sat nearby, watching the proceedings while panting contentedly. *What a bastard dog*, thought Gabriel.

"I heard that," said Payne, who had yet to regain his clean, regal form. He still looked and smelled like a dead and rotting animal.

"Mabel's my best friend, so please give her due respect."

Gabriel could only muster a grunting noise in reply.

"And by the way, my fine, tickled friend, you most definitely do belong here! Because, as a matter of harsh fact, you wouldn't be here if you didn't!"

Gabriel thought for a brief moment then spat back, "I don't belong here! I was a good kid! There's been a terrible error!"

"Give it a rest," growled Mabel, and Gabriel's attention was riveted to the talking dog, who here-to-fore had only been a barking and yapping dog, as are the only type Gabriel's ever been witness to.

But Gabriel's shock faded quickly, being used to this type of thing in hell, and he hatched a plan in an instant, without really thinking about it, so Payne was none the wiser.

"I don't belong here!" Gabriel shouted.

Payne and Mabel both rolled their eyes.

"I don't belong here! Send me to heaven!"

Payne continued his evil deeds, but he grimaced as he tickled.

So in this fashion did Gabriel continue, crying foul every few moments or so, begging to be released from hell. He knew his plan was a long shot, but at the very least he hoped to give back a little bit of what he was getting.

Payne began to think to himself whilst tickling Gabriel's feet, trying mightily to block out the kid's irksome demands. *Shut up, kid! Shut up! Arrrghhh! You're actually getting under MY skin! Not many have the ability to do that! Screams of pain and torment I enjoy! I can listen to them for hours on end; sweet music to my ears. But listening to a snotty kid complain to me? That's unacceptable! Ugghhh. Shut up!*

He paused his thoughts, then:

Don't think you belong here, kid? Okay. We'll see if you belong here or not!

It was then that Payne hatched *his* plan, to take Gabriel to see the big man, because, if Payne knew anything, it was that the big man's time and attention were not to be trifled with, and he was always in a most foul mood. The Devil would punish Gabriel mightily indeed, once he heard his absurd claim to not "belonging" here. He laughed to himself. *This'll be great!*

Payne stopped the feather and a smile filled his face. "I'll tell you what," he addressed Gabriel. Mabel looked at her master with confusion and a tilted head.

"Maybe you're right."

Mabel's head tilted even further, and she let out a small whine.

"Maybe you're not supposed to be here."

Mabel barked angrily at her master.

"Calm down!" he shot at Mabel, in a sinister and angry fashion. She yelped passively in obedience. Payne turned his attention back to Gabriel.

"This is what we're going to do." Gabriel was impassive. "I'm going to take you to the only being I know of who can make the determination of whether or not you belong here."

Gabriel's heart managed a small but cautious leap.

"I'm going to take you to my boss. The big man. Satan."

Gabriel's heart sunk back down immediately.

Mabel began to regain her composure, and a smile began to form on her canine lips. She realized what Payne was up to. Gabriel noticed the happy dog, and he began to fret. *This isn't good*, he thought to himself. *I've made things worse.*

"Oh, please," replied Payne. "Don't worry. You may just get your wish!"

Gabriel couldn't help but notice the telling smirks on the faces of both of his tormentors. *I'm in for it, now*, he lamented to himself.

So off the three of them set as before, the moribund troopers, with Payne taking the lead, Mabel close at his side, and a floating Gabriel taking up the rear. This break in the action gave Gabriel time to reflect, but it began to occur to him that thinking, as he was used to defining it, was simply not possible anymore. The shock of his torture and the reading of his mind had trained him, much to his chagrin, to use his brain as little as possible. He'd come to the disheartening conclusion that he simply couldn't think anymore, at least not to the degree that he was used to. He felt depressed. He tried his best to put this out of his head—which wasn't as hard as it should've been—and he resumed feeling like a tub of jello.

He noticed something in the distance, for the very first time.

Seemed to be a line of trees. *A forest in hell?* Gabriel wondered.

"No, I don't think so," came Payne's snotty retort. Gabriel glumly readied himself for whatever it was. Fact was though, it was quite far away, and it took another few hours of trodding this barren wasteland before Gabriel could get a clearer look at what he was seeing. Still looked like trees to him, though. They had a trunk, and what seemed to be a bushy top, and they swayed slightly in the breeze, although it occurred to Gabriel that there was no breeze, and never had been, here in the land of empty yellowness.

Mabel turned and growled. "They're not trees!"

Whatever they were, Gabriel and his "pals" were headed straight into the meat of them. And when they reached the edge of the massive, strange forest, Gabriel realized that his tormentors were right—of course—and they weren't trees at all. In fact, they were jellyfish, or something quite similar, floating together as if languishing lazily in an invisible sea. *Bizarre,* thought Gabriel.

Payne laughed under his breath. Gabriel thought he heard Mabel doing the same, as the cryptic canine shot a quick glance back to Payne. Gabriel braced himself for the worst, and the two beings pulled him, like a frightened kite, into the forest of jellyfish.

Payne and Mabel were careful. They easily side-stepped all who swayed in their direction. Gabriel, however, didn't have such luck. Being helplessly yanked forward, he bounced from angry jellyfish to angrier jellyfish, receiving white-hot stings to his entire body from the flailing, grasping tentacles of the menacing creatures. He wanted to pass out from the pain, but as he'd come to suspect, this would not be allowed.

Sting after sting. Shock after shock. Like a dentist's drill to his spinal column. Pus-filled welts arose from his exposed places.

Here and there, through his swollen eyelids and watering eyes, he was able to spy Payne and Mabel looking his way and laughing hard. Laughing really hard! *These creatures really are incredibly evil*, it occurred to Gabriel more indelibly than before. *What kind of heinous behavior did they perpetrate when they were on earth?*

"We've never been to earth!" came the smarmy retort from Mabel. "What a horrible place!" Mabel then shot Payne a wide smile and they burst out laughing once more. Gabriel didn't see the comedy, but he did look up ahead just in time to see the forest of jellyfish thinning out in front of him.

The three of them seemed to have come upon a clearing, actually, and in the very middle of this forest, the odd, yellowish ground took a dip, almost as if it were being sucked down a drain. The closer they got, the larger Gabriel realized this hole was. It seemed alive, and was pulling in energy from all around it. Gabriel thought of a television show he'd seen on cable not too long ago about black holes, and how they bend space and time in a similar way. This reminded him of that.

"You know, kid, you really are much too smart for your own good," admonished Payne. Gabriel—scorched, red, and swollen as he was—replied to Payne with a non-caring glare.

"Come now, my little friend! Don't be so glum," Payne added. "The fun's just begun!"

Inexorably, the three made their way toward the hole, and the closer they came, the more their very matter began to pull apart, so that Payne's right foot, for instance, entered the hole long before his left foot did. Suddenly, the distance between the tip of Gabriel's nose and his upper lip seemed to be miles, as they slid down this chute. *This is a black hole!* Gabriel concluded.

"I never said you weren't smart, kid," were Payne's last words in this particular universe, while at the very same moment Gabriel caught a quick glance over the event horizon of the jellyfish that he was leaving behind. But they weren't jellyfish after all, he realized. They were tortured, human souls.

THE MONSTER'S LAIR

IN WHAT SEEMED to be both an infinitely small amount of time and also the longest duration—near infinity—that Gabriel'd ever experienced, the three intrepid travelers found themselves in a dank, dark cave. Gabriel was no longer floating, so he turned this way and that, to inspect the place. It was furnished, actually, in a most Victorian fashion. And as Gabriel's eyes became used to the light, he realized that the place actually had an air of quaintness and civility. A charm, if you will.

It was then that he remembered his flagellation by the jellyfish forest of tormented souls, and it surprised him to realize that he was no longer in pain. So he inspected himself, and to his delight, he lacked the swollen membranes and red, burning welts that he'd just incurred (or was it eons ago?). Regardless, it was a pleasant turn of events in an otherwise bleak parade of misfortune.

"Don't get cocky, kid," Payne reminded. He was back to his human, well-dressed self, and he was nervously eyeballing an unremarkable, green door. Mabel was watching it too, and was twitching with the need to yelp in excitement, and it was clearly all she could do to keep from not.

Since Payne and Mabel were waiting for something, Gabriel took the time to look around and inspect the abode more closely. It was filled with artifacts from many different eras of human existence, apparently, and there were even things that didn't seem human at all. There were pieces of Neanderthal cave paintings hanging from the ceiling. Gabriel recognized those from his studies. He noticed a genuine, Peruvian shrunken head, and a marble sculpture of a young man from the classical Greek period.

Assuming that this was Satan's lair, as Gabriel was doing, it made perfect sense that he'd have collected interesting items throughout the history of his tormenting the human race.

There were jars of medical oddities setting near Tiffany lamps and even Tupperware. Tupperware? *Whatever*, thought Gabriel.

Beautiful, deep hued fabrics were draped in every corner, and everything seem lit from below, creating a very cozy and interesting feel. Gabriel couldn't be sure, but it seemed as if this light was from flames. Made sense.

Oddly, there were no chairs, but there were a few finely hewn tables, each from antiquated origin, no doubt. Art filled every wall, from Renaissance masterpieces to abstract, angry modern things. In fact, the more Gabriel looked, the more it seemed as if the art actually made the walls, and the orange-hued light streamed through the cracks between, creating quite the creepy atmosphere.

Gabriel was fixating on the yellow glow of a tabled, jewel-like trinket, when he heard a creaking sound. He look up to see the innocuous green door begin to slowly open, then spied Payne and Mabel both genuflecting toward said door in a most extreme fashion. The form of a figure began to take shape in the shadows of the door as it swung open. And just as Gabriel's brain was about to comprehend what it was he was seeing, a bright red flash filled his vision, and his brain with pain. When he recovered a few milliseconds later, he was most shocked to see that he was in the backseat of an automobile. When he attempted to look this way and that to make sense of his new surroundings, he realized that he was constrained. A quick look down and a flood of recognition of the car seat drew him to the conclusion that he was an infant buckled into a child's seat, and he was indeed in his family's auto of yore.

"Where am I?" Gabriel screamed to the driver of the vehicle.

Unfortunately for the driver, however, Gabriel's query sounded more like a baby screaming in discontent, which was precisely what it was. And Gabriel knew it too.

The driver glared back at Gabriel, and sternly said, "Quiet! That's enough!"

Gabriel nearly shat his pants when he realized that it was his father driving the car. And not only was his father highly agitated, his eyes were glazed over with fear. And this fear spread to baby Gabriel, prompting him to say something to his scared father. Anything. But once again, his voice spit from his mouth as nothing more than screaming and crying incoherence, and his father responded in kind by shouting back at him, which in turn only elicited more screaming from infant Gabriel.

It was in the middle of this scream-fest that Gabriel heard a series of loud pops, the shattering of glass, felt a sudden lurch, the squeal of tires, and the thud of his father's head into the windshield. In an instance after the chaos, silence ruled, not the least of which was the lack of any sound whatsoever from his father. The silence was broken by a violent tugging at his father's car door. It thrust open, and a man in black, wearing sunglasses, thrust his head into the car. He was holding a gun. He squared his stare with Gabriel's eyes. Gabriel heard a click, then began to scream and cry mightily, but before he knew it, he was back in the Devil's Den, looking up at the Devil himself, whipping tears from his eyes.

"Wow. I'm pretty good, aren't I?" said Satan. "Even these numbskulls"—pointing to Payne and Mabel—"can't do stuff like that."

Payne and Mabel arched their humble spines even more than seemed possible in response to their master's jab.

"So your father's dead…Hmmm…I wonder if he's down here somewhere."

The Devil tilted his head back and his eyes began to spin like tops. Gabriel looked on and beheld this evil of all evils. He was large—of course—like a sumo wrestler, but not as fat. Built more like a football player, really.

He was wearing a suit and tie, albeit of a deep, rich red color. His skin was lime green, and it was hard to ignore the fact that he had four arms. His face was not unlike a Japanese mask of kabuki fame, with deep fissures and intense emotions streaming across his visage in rapid succession. And he had three horns. That seemed the oddest to Gabriel. One on each side of the head as one might expect, but a third right in the middle of his forehead, not unlike a unicorn.

His eyes spun to a stop and he looked down at Gabriel. "It's the horns, isn't it? The three horns. Nobody but nobody expects that. Silly Renaissance artists. And they thought they were being clever…"

"Uh…well…" managed Gabriel.

"Unfortunately, your father is nowhere to be found down here. Rats."

"Um…eh…I…" Gabriel creaked again.

"OKAY!" came the booming command, and Payne and Mabel both shot upright to attention, trembling all the while.

"Let's get this show on the road!" Satan's voice began to fill with rumbling and anger, and even Gabriel began to quake a bit.

"SPEAK!" Satan bellowed at Payne.

"Master! Master!" he was able to stammer. "My charge Gabriel here insists that there's been a terrible mistake, and he doesn't belong here in hell!"

Mabel began to snicker, seeing the punishment headed Gabriel's way.

The evil one gained a thoughtful countenance and turned away to think. As he plodded through his crowed chateau, an errant elbow bumped the small yellow jewel] that Gabriel had been fascinated with earlier. It clanged to the ground, but Satan was none the wiser, since he was deep in thought. His back still turned, he spoke.

"Doesn't belong here, eh?"

Mabel gave Payne a confused glare. She had expected fireworks by now, not contemplation.

"Well, I don't know about that, really," continued Satan.

Payne returned Mabel's look of confusion in kind.

Satan muttered on, and Gabriel took the opportunity to rescue the fallen trinket. He stepped forward, picked it up, and set it gingerly on the table from which it had dropped. The Devil turned immediately, fixated on Gabriel with a face nearly filled with anger, but not quite. Mabel and Payne relaxed, happy that Gabriel was finally about to get his.

"He's right!" Satan boomed. "He most definitely does not belong here!"

You could have heard a pin drop in the hearts of Satan's two little helpers.

"Doesn't belong here?" Payne spat, in a gross breach of protocol. "How can you possib—" A sudden realization of the errors of his ways, brought about by a ridicu-lously stern stare-down from his master, ended Payne's outburst. In fact, steam had begun to rise from Satan's green, glowing head. A sight to behold in fear, if there ever was one.

Once Bip and Bap had resumed their submissive bows in respectful silence, the Evil One cleared his throat and addressed Gabriel directly.

"As odd as it may seem, young man," he began, "You're right. You don't belong here."

On Gabriel's mouth began the makings of a smile, for the first time since his ordeal began. Satan continued:

"That became clear to me the moment you picked up my grandmum's amulet. Consideration like that is absent from souls tainted by evil. Plus, I did a quick scan of the Records of the Damned, and you're not listed. A pity, but I'll have plenty of torturing to occupy myself here for a long, long time, believe me."

Gabriel's proto-smile morphed into a real, albeit small and tentative, smile.

"How you ended up here, I can't be sure, but this type of thing has been known to happen." Satan shot Payne and his dog a look of exasperation. "I guess Payne has never had the misfortune of encountering this type of thing before. A hard lesson to learn for a couple of prideful yet loyal fools. Death dealing can be hard." Mabel whimpered like a scolded pooch.

And then, much to Gabriel's surprise, Satan's body disappeared, and where his head had been, a cat slowly took its place, until instead of a large-bodied demon holding court, there was but a green and purple cat floating in midair.

"Come here," the cat commanded Gabriel, who began to float up toward the new demonic visage. The cat was holding a small piece of paper in his left paw and he handed it to a confused Gabriel.

"Here you go."

"Uh…thanks…" mumbled Gabe, as he took the paper.

"Any last words for the master of the underworld, Gabriel?" the cat said, with a very cat-like voice.

Gabriel thought for an absent-minded moment, then: "Well, it's good to know that my father's in heaven." Gabriel began to rise again, and as he looked down upon the shrinking scene below him, the cat-shaped Satan replied, "I don't know where he is, kid. All I know is, he's not down here…"

These words reverberated oddly and uncomfortably in Gabriel's head as he rose higher and higher, toward the roof of Satan's lair. He thought he caught a last glimpse of Payne and Mabel, both glaring at him with all the hate they could muster, before he slipped through the roof and into the damned, infinite cavern most foul that was hell proper. Everywhere around him was red-tinged darkness and pain and heat and fire, yet he continued his rise to freedom, getting what he realized was a privileged tour of the underworld that most condemned souls would never have.

He looked at the piece of paper in his hand. It was an important looking little certificate, with frilly borders and odd, calligraphic writing. Gabriel couldn't read the writing at first, as it seemed an alien language; indeed, but after a moment, somehow it became English. *Odd,* Gabriel thought. It read:

"The Bearer of this Document, one Gabriel Ellis McGregor, is Now and Forever given the Right to Leave Hell. Signed, Beelzebub, the Destroyer of Worlds."

Wow, thought Gabriel. *I actually got out of hell! Oh… wait a second…*

Gabriel had spotted a disclaimer in small type:

"Should the bearer return to Hell for any reason, however, this passport no longer applies. No exceptions."

Well, that's okay, Gabriel reasoned, *'cos I ain't coming back here again!*

Tis true that Gabriel's surroundings were still most unwelcoming, but the very fact that he was leaving this place put a smile in Gabriel's heart for the first time in a long while. And as he floated higher, still, his mind relaxed, and he seemed to regain his ability to think and reason again. *A most pleasant development,* he thought to himself.

Still, all around him was the heat and the smell of forever-death, and although that which he was leaving behind was shrinking into a bird's-eye view below him, he knew he still had a few moments left in hell. He thought about how exactly he was going to leave this place. Would he have to present his pass to some sort of gatekeeper? Would he wake up in his bed, in his body, none the worse for wear? Or would he be sent to heaven, where he knew he deserved to go? *Either way would be okay*, Gabriel surmised. Sure he'd miss his family and friends if he went to heaven, but if he was really and truly dead, no sense quibbling, because heaven's gotta be the coolest of places, right?

Gabriel looked up to see where he was headed exactly. His heart skipped a beat when he spied the same upside-down, stalactite cityscape that he'd passed on the way down. This worried Gabriel a bit, because he knew it'd be crawling with unsavory denizens. Hopefully, there was someone there waiting for him to send him on his way—a magistrate of some sort. An evil magistrate, though probably. *Oh, dear.*

Gabriel's fears did not come to pass for the first time in his sojourn. He did see many strange and horrid creatures as he floatingly entered the upside-down city, but they ignored him totally—even seemed to fear him—as he noticed their goings on.

There were plenty of humans of course—as bedeviled and bedraggled as humans can be—but there were other odd creatures scampering about the hanging spires and crooked, desperate houses that held them. Mostly, these creatures looked spider-like, with pseudo-human heads, but without the hair you'd expect on a spider. More like a naked human with eight legs? *Yuck!* Gabriel thought, appropriately enough.

Plus, there were tall, lanky, human-like creatures that seemed to have only half a body. That is, they only sported either one left arm and accompanying left leg, or one right and left leg. They hopped on whatever single foot that they owned, and their bald heads were scarred and inflamed. *Most unsavory!* Gabriel felt. He could make these judgments now easily, because he was leaving this spectacle behind for good. If he was destined to live among them for eternity, well then, he'd have a much heavier heart about the whole thing.

He looked up, and the street of the upside-down city was rapidly approaching. As he touched down, head first, it was if he was in water and the street above him was an ice sheet keeping him under. In other words, from the point of view of the denizens of this bizarre place, Gabriel was walking down the street on his head, a quite talented circus trick, indeed.

Gabriel felt confused. He had no idea where to go. All around him was the upside-down oddness of scurrying, scary feet, and his universe had been reduced to the trash and flotsam and jetsam that covered the public walkways of the upside-down section of hell. A disgusting site to survey so closely to be sure.

Figuring that there had to be an obvious way out, Gabriel walked—handstand-walked, as it were—in whatever direction seemed appropriate. After an hour or so, he began to get a little exasperated. But after what he'd just been through, he figured a little patience would do him good. It was at that moment that a bald, scarred, and highly unsavory face popped into Gabriel's upside-down view, with nary an inch or so for personal space. Gabriel jumped.

"That's what yer lookin' fer, I'm quite sure," the demon rasped, as if his throat had been shredded with a large, rat-tail file. He was pointing to what seemed to be a manhole cover in the middle of the street. Gabriel tried to squeak out some sort of appreciative reply, but the creature had vanished as quickly as it came.

Gabriel hand-walked his way over to the manhole cover, and beheld it in detail. At first glance, it looked like any other manhole cover, but on closer inspection, the language it held was in the same script as was written on his pass from hell. A moment later, he could read it. It said:

"Remove this manhole at the peril of your soul."

"Hmmm…" Gabriel considered. Then he spotted some fine print.

"Holders of an A12-Q459Y-EX44 exit pass are exempted and can pass."

"Hmmm!" Gabriel realized. He looked over his pass, and sure enough, on the back and in small print, he saw the code that he was looking for. He read it, but was chagrined to see that it didn't quite match. He was holding an A12-Q459Y-EX44-*G* pass!

That's got to be the same thing! Gabriel convinced himself. *I mean, that stupid little G can't matter, right?* He was deep into rationalization, now. But he was desperate to leave, so who could blame him?

He considered the ramifications of holding the wrong pass, and what might happen if he tried to use this exit without proper authorization. *Could be a* BIG *mistake. Are there more of these exits? Does each one require a different coded pass? Will I have to search for hours, days or months for the right one?* Something snapped in Gabriel's brain. He could take no more of this absurd silliness, and he lifted the manhole in a quick and decisive manner, consequences be damned (no pun intended). And as his hopes had hoped he would, he floated through the hole without a problem, and he'd finally left hell behind. The pass, it turned out, was the right one.

THE LINGERING LOST

GABRIEL PRESUMED THAT, upon leaving hell, he was going to find himself smack-dab in the middle of heaven, or at the very least, alive and back on earth somehow. After all, where else was there to be? All he'd ever been taught about such matters involved no more than the three realms of earth, heaven, and hell. And since he'd lived on earth and been sent to, and ejected from, hell, his next stop would be heaven. The prospect excited him, definitely, but so did returning to his family on earth. *Either would suffice*, he told himself, as he took in his new surroundings. His new surroundings, however, disappointed him greatly.

A shiver of realization shot up Gabriel's spine. He'd left hell only seconds ago, and yet he was already certain that he was still far away from anywhere that he wished to be. Fear enveloped him as he understood that he had absolutely no idea where he was, and as such was as lost as a person can be.

He looked himself over, closely inspecting himself. His body, clothing, shoes; everything seemed to be in order, but Gabriel concluded, instinctively, that he was still Gabriel in spirit, not body. He steeled himself for more adventure ahead, thrust his jaw forward a bit, and began to inspect this new, unfamiliar place.

He was, for lack of a better description, inside an endless tunnel that seemed to resemble the insides of a gigantic submarine, as much as anything else. It was cold here too, Gabriel quickly realized. And gray and metallic, with humming noises of a seemingly mechanical nature, emanating from the very fabric of the place. Ugly fluorescent lights fought darkness, and here and there blue, red, and green lights carved out corners between pipes and fittings and bulkheads. As he took a step, the clank of his shoe brought his attention to the floor and to the metal grating that lined the bottom of the tunnel for as far as the eye could see.

Gabriel stopped and thought for a moment.

He looked to his right, and the tunnel stretched on seemingly forever. He looked to his left, and the vision was the same. However, there seemed to be an exit not too far down, so he considered his options. *Best see where that goes*, he thought to himself, and he struck off toward it.

He wasn't but a few moments into his new journey when he heard a noise that caught his attention. Froze him in his tracks, actually, as it seemed to be the moaning of a person, hidden from view.

Gabriel glanced about, but saw no one.

"Over here…" The moan was carrying syllables.

It seemed to be coming from ahead, so he stepped forward gingerly, searching every nook and cranny he could spy.

"Here!" came the urgent, gravelly directive. Then Gabriel saw some movement a few feet forward. An elbow poking out of the darkness? He carefully approached, and as he stepped forward, a whole person seemed to appear from nothing, as if birthed by the black from which he was hiding. Gabriel stopped, stunned. This specter wasn't a happy fellow, that's for sure, as his clothing could pass for layers of gray, tattered rags, and his face was buried in a beard and mustache the likes of a mountain man. He came out of his hiding place crooked, either unable or unwilling to stand.

"Hello," Gabriel managed.

"Who are you?" came the confused reply.

"I…"

"You have no business here!" was the brusque, angry retort.

"Well, I…"

"Do I care?" The man's tone was suddenly one of defeat. "You can do whatever you want. But you won't *want* to do anything, is the funny thing…"

That last bit caught Gabriel by surprise. "I…uh…"

"Go away!" shouted the man, and he disappeared into his dark corner as quickly as he had appeared.

Gabriel thought he heard him mutter, "No one cares, anyway…"

Gabriel stepped past the wretch and his cold, dark corner, and the man seemed to melt into his surroundings, much like a salamander's skin would do. He considered asking him a few important questions, but thought better of it. Big, ugly, pinkish-green fluorescent lights buzzed overhead and into Gabriel's ears. He thought he could hear an engine powering up somewhere, but couldn't be sure. Was he on some sort of ship? Or in the bowels of a giant building? His head began to spin, but then stopped dead on this potent thought: *I'm not in hell anymore, so at least that's something.* Gabriel steeled his nerves, and pushed on.

Clank, clank, clank, went the soles of his shoes against the metal grating that lined the floor of this never-ending hallway. Moans of displeasure wafted from left and right into Gabriel's ears; his head turning on swivel to see from where they emanated, but all he'd spy were folks like the first man he'd encountered. Tattered grey beings ever so slightly visible in their dark, dank cubbyholes, with nary but the whites of their eyes and teeth showing through.

The moans seemed to be directed toward Gabriel as his presence seemed to be causing a bit of a stir as he walked, but Gabriel found it easy to ignore these sounds of sorrow, since it was clear that these pitiful creatures had not the energy to say much to him, let alone do him any harm. Gabriel'd come this far and was quite determined to get the hell out of this place, just like the last. He'd find a way; he was certain of this, so on he went.

Gabriel stopped at a crossroads of sorts. To his left was another impossibly long hallway jutting toward who knows where. To his right was a doorway. Gabriel was excited to see the door as he often felt doors are a passageway to something better, but his heart sank when he read the dozens of warning signs that were painting the thing: Keep Out, Danger, Radiation Zone, Authorized Entry Only, Deadly Force Authorized for Trespassers, etcetera.

Gabriel got the picture. It wasn't a good idea to open the door. All right already. Besides, the handle—large, round, and mounted to many levers and gears—seemed only workable by someone five times Gabriel's size and quadruple his strength, at least. So, Gabriel headed down the hallway to the left, hoping to find something new.

But he didn't. In fact, it was quite more of the same. Endlessly the same. More moaning, grey "people"; more awful, loud, and ugly fluorescent lights above head; more low frequency rumbling beneath his feet; and—except when stopping to inspect the occasional curiosity—more clanking of his shoes against the grating. And grating the whole thing was. Very grating to Gabriel's nerves. And then Gabriel noticed a shift inside himself. His steely, confident chin fell slack and weak. He realized suddenly that he was very, very tired.

And he was beginning, ever so slightly, to believe that he'd never get out of this place. In fact, it was beginning to dawn on him that he very well may still be in hell proper. *What a depressing thought*, thought Gabriel. And it was depressing, indeed, since thinking it sent him into quite the little depression.

Gabriel did the logical thing and sat down. He sat down and began to wallow in his new depression. Somehow in an odd way, thought Gabriel, it felt good to wallow in depression. *And I have quite a lot to be depressed about, I do.* So he wallowed, and continued to wallow still, with each wallowing making him more depressed, and then ever more eager to wallow further. This behavior seemed right to him, somehow.

Gabriel leaned back and noticed that he was but a few butt scootches from a nice, cool, dark nook, away from the glare and sound of the fluorescent lights. He moved himself backwards and relaxed finally as his back slid up against the cool metal of the hallway, darkness and coolness enveloping him. For once in a long while, he actually felt a little safe. He could breathe easy.

"GET OUT OF MY SPACE!" came the screeching. And indeed Gabriel did. For the shock sent him shooting from his comfortable spot like a spring-loaded frog. Gabriel turned to see a shell of a human—this one quite angry—giving him the "what for," but for only a brief, passion-filled moment; then the passion was gone, and the thing slipped back into the hole from whence it came, as if nothing had transpired.

Gabriel's heart was beating out of his chest, and the adrenalin did him good. Suddenly, his depression lifted a bit—just a bit, but enough to realize his plight once more, and to try and figure a solution.

Once again, *clank clank clank* went his footfalls, but his time with less urgency. He was moving and searching, but still under the spell of this depressing place. He was looking for an exit, but also, in the back of his mind, looking for his own little cool and dark safe haven.

Onward he walked, seemingly forever. The hallway never ended, never deviated from perfectly straight, never altered its shape or lighting or sounds or smell. Until he came to the next crossroads, after what seemed like days. Same as the last: hallway to the left, off-limits doorway to the right.

Try as he might, Gabriel couldn't bring up the energy to even consider trying to open the door. A very, very small part of him knew it was the thing to do— against all appearances—but the rest of him was convinced it'd be an exercise in disaster, as all the warnings told him so. He was feeling more depressed suddenly. He turned on his heels and headed down the hallway straight across from the door, just as he did at the last intersection. Seemed logical somehow. Seemed meaningless too, in a meaningful way. Oddly, this all made sense to Gabriel.

Clank, clank, clank.

Gabriel was walking, but trudging was more like it: slowly, depressingly, one foot after the other. He looked down at himself and noticed that his clothing had somehow become tattered and grey, and he felt old somehow, even though old isn't even in the vocabulary of an eleven-year-old.

A hand reached out and grabbed his right ankle. Gabriel barely flinched, he was so low.

"Stop," said the voice.

Gabriel searched up the arm to see who was attached to it, and it was a woman, maybe. It was hard to tell.

"Excuse me?" Gabriel replied.

"Stop. Go no further, or you will never leave. That's all...I...can..." her voice trailed off.

Her hand released Gabriel's ankle and slid back into darkness. Gabriel stood there, confused and a little stunned, and suddenly became belligerent. "Then what am I supposed to do? Huh?"

No reply.

Gabriel was getting heated, now. "I mean, what else is there to do? Go back? Why? Go forward? Who cares?"

"The... door..."

"The door? You mean the impossible-to-open door? The you're-going-to-die-if-you-open-it door? Oh yeah! That door!"

The woman's hand reappeared, and pointed in the direction from whence Gabriel'd come. "I realize, now...the...door...Don't be like..."

"What?" Gabriel was pissed.

No reply.

"Like what?" Veins were bulging on Gabriel's brow, now.

"Like...me..." Her hand disappeared, and in fact, she did in her entirety as far as Gabriel could see.

The extra dose of adrenalin from his anger put a small skip in Gabriel's step, and thinking he had nothing to lose, except for retracing what seemed like years of walking, he decided to head back toward that damn door.

Head back, he did, but finding the energy to keep going turned out to be a vexing proposition, indeed. If his feet had previously felt as if they were trudging through molasses, then now they seemed almost glued to the metal grating by a strong magnetic tug. It was as if someone or something was trying to tell Gabriel: "This course of action is folly! Please turn back!"

But that very resistance made Gabriel realize, if only for a moment, that he must in actuality be doing the right thing. For surely, in this land, that which seemed wrong on the surface must actually be the right thing to do. At least, the momentary arrival of this thought kept him going forward just that bit more, until drained of energy, at which point this same thought would reappear—as if thought for the first time—giving Gabriel just the right amount of juice to push ahead again.

Finally, he saw it. The Door. The *you-better-not-open-this-butthead* Door. And as each step toward it became ever more impossibly hard to make—like trying to push two magnets of different poles together—

his focus on the door and all that it might grant him tunnel-visioned into a laser sharpness, to the point of blocking out all that surrounded him—all was the door.

And as he approached the door, in the final few feet of distance, denizens of this realm—long lost to the permanence of their plight—began to reach from their cloistered darkness and grabbed at Gabriel's small legs, moaning for him to stop.

"NOOOOO!" they moaned. "You'll kill us all!" they added. "You mustn't!" was their final counsel.

But a funny thing happened. Even though each push forward was torturous for Gabriel—especially with a group of eternally sad souls tugging at his extremities—an odd energy began to bubble up from the base of his spine, and as it traveled up his body, strength began to return to his frame.

Finally only inches away, he grabbed the large, round handle of the thing, and as he began to turn it, his strength increased even more, much to his surprise and delight: and to just as much dismay to those poor sods trying to prevent his escape. In fact, as Gabriel's strength and energy grew, so did the volume of the moaning and groaning and horrid protestations, and the vehemence of the tugs at his body. But this just underscored in Gabriel's mind that he was definitely doing the right thing. It was almost as if his strength was feeding off of their fear; and they'd grown by the dozens, by the way. It was as if all of the inhabitants of this place had come to stop Gabriel's departure. The scene had become a gigantic chaotic cacophony of distress and fear, deeply layered around a fine, bright light of strength and determination at the very center. They were trying their best to snuff this out—to make Gabriel like them, but by now Gabriel felt as if he was the Hulk, and nothing could stop him. And, indeed, even though those last few moments of turning the handle counter-clockwise and listening to the latches unbolt, along with the shrieks and moans of fear that was incredibly loud in Gabriel's ear, seemed to take years to transpire, he was for all intents and purposes Sampson for that one shining moment, and he completed his mission. The door unlatched; a bright, beautiful light shown through; the hundreds of frightful souls that had piled upon Gabriel's back were blown away, back to their fear-soaked hovels; and Gabriel was sucked through the doorway quickly; it slamming shut behind him. Out of the corner of his eye, he caught a dank dweller or two take the same leap he did, but he couldn't be sure, since they seemed to disappear into thin air. Regardless, Gabriel was through, and he was standing in the midst of one of the most beautiful meadows he'd ever been witness too. The sky was crystalline blue, the clouds were perfectly puffy, and the hills beyond rambled emerald-green into the distance. *This must be Heaven*, Gabriel mused.

THE VALLEY OF THE GORGE

GABRIEL TURNED AROUND. The doorway he'd just been thrust through was gone. Not a single sign of where he'd been, remained. Just endless, blissful hills, and grass and trees and butterflies, and billowy cloud-filled sunny skies as far as he could see. Without thinking, he let out the biggest, longest sigh he'd ever let. Relaxation, finally! Aaaahhhhh…

As was his recent acquired habit upon arriving at a new interdimensional destination, he gave himself a quick once over. Not surprisingly, his clothes were no longer tattered—his outfit was quite fit, as if washed and pressed during the transition between extra-dimensional planes. Tailored, seemingly, too. Fashionable, even, as far as an eleven-year-old could understand fashion. Either way, Gabriel felt dressed appropriately for the occasion, whatever occasion this place had placed him into. Or something like that.

Being nowhere in particular, but quite comfortable and relaxed, and not just a little bit energized by his new surroundings, Gabriel decided to walk. There seemed nothing much more to do than that at the moment, and being that every direction contained the same vista, he randomly chose the direction that seemed in some odd, instinctive way like "North" to him. And "North," to Gabriel, always seemed a more proper direction than the rest.

Walk, he did. And walk and walk, some more. Oddly, the sun held at the top of the sky while hours passed, not moving a bit from its perch, but that felt right. *If this was Heaven*, Gabriel thought. He was quite enjoying his explorations, actually, as he came across many an interesting insect crawling along the ground from large, red ants to bright purple and pink fuzzy caterpillars. Unlike his backyard at home, these bugs weren't trying to eat each other, and really seemed to only be doing precisely what Gabriel was—enjoying exploring their surroundings.

A three-inch, dark-blue millipede with heavy armor and large, angry-looking pincers walked right across a lazy, bug-eyed slug and didn't even stop to take a bite. The slug didn't mind the intrusion a bit! How odd, but very pleasing, felt Gabriel.

He dug into the dirt between the sprouts of short fescue and brought up clods filled with franticly twisting psychedelically-hued beetles and wriggling, dark purple earth worms. *The fishing I could do with these guys!* he mused. Setting the bugs back to their ground, he noticed that the knees of his pants wouldn't even take stain from the grass and dirt. *This place would certainly be Heaven for my mom!* Gabriel joked to himself.

Gabriel stood and noticed something odd in the distance. On a hillside, there looked to be growing from the ground small mounds as if things were rising from below. There were dozens of these grassy little points, and they were gaining height alarmingly fast, casting shadows as they grew. Even more alarmingly, dozens more sprouted, then, as if a wave; more and more, filling the ground between Gabriel and the hill, until Gabriel was actually standing in the midst of these rising columns of grass and dirt. All this happened in but a few breaths' time, making retreat impossible.

Disconcertingly, they stopped growing at about the height of an average adult human, and then, as if on cue, every one of them, as far as Gabriel could see, transformed into a jolly and festive man or woman, wearing nothing but Roman togas.

Instantly, Gabriel was encased in the hubbub and to-do of a large gathering, filled to the brim with catching up and chit chat and back slapping aplenty. Overwhelmed a bit was Gabriel, being that just moments previous, he'd been the most relaxed and content that he may have ever been—ever—due to the profound and beautiful silence that he was enjoying. That silence was gone. He was now smack-dab in the middle of a large town party.

A hefty toga-ed man looked down and spotted Gabriel.

"Well, hello, little one! I don't recognize you! You from around here?"

"Hello," came Gabriel's furtive reply. He was a little bowled over by the man's intense enthusiasm. It was good news though, that the man was certainly in a pleasant mood, as was everyone else it seemed.

"Hmmm," the man continued, leaning down and fingering the lining of Gabriel's left sleeve. "Odd clothes. Never seen anything like this around these parts! You're definitely not from here!" He laughed uproariously, just to do it. Gabriel chuckled in reply. "Doesn't matter. You seem a good sort! And you're just in time for the festivities!"

"Festivit-eh?"

"Festivities, young fellow! Here. Let me show you!"

The man bent down further, grabbed Gabriel around the waist, and in an instant, Gabriel was sitting on the man's shoulders, with only unfamiliar hair and ears to grab to steady himself. He was now higher than anyone else, and Gabriel was amazed that everywhere, in all directions as far as he could see, was a sea of people—of all stripes, colors, sizes, and shapes; all draped in white, sun-drenched togas—carpeting the hills that had only moments previous been lush, green, and quiet. The difference a moment makes!

And just about then, a large commotion swelled through the crowd, like a wave of emotion; it was excitement bottled in roars of anticipation. It was clear to Gabriel that something interesting was about to transpire, and sure enough in the midst of the crowd, circular pockets of space appeared, like droplets of water swelling in a puddle of oil. The masses were pulling back—letting something in, as if creating room for a landing craft, but instead, things came up from below and filled the round, emerging spaces: large tables filled with food of any and all imaginable kind. An incredible display of culinary variety! It'd been so long since Gabriel'd eaten that the food-stuffs seemed almost alien, and he'd nearly forgotten how to react. His hunger response had been dead, and still, even witnessing this wonton display of gigantic amounts of glorious eats from a distance, he could barely even manage the slightest sensation of hunger. But it wasn't the same for everyone else, for Gabriel now felt as if he was riding an elephant, running for a rare water hole in deep thirst. He bounced like a cowboy hanging onto a bronco for dear life, as his charge charged the nearest giant table of mountainous food and shouted with glee, just like everyone trundling at his fore and aft. It was really a frightening display of unbridled passion. *Must be really good food!* Gabriel mused, between bumps and thumps.

Upon arrival at the table, the man set Gabriel down in a most terse and unceremonious fashion, much to Gabriel's chagrin—especially considering how friendly he was but a moment earlier. *No friend is he*, Gabriel mused. He then suffered a fate similar to a bowling pin's, being bounced about un-mercilessly by the thighs and buttocks of the hunger-possessed that tightly surrounded him, as their behavior now mimicked craven dogs fighting for each other's part of a kill. *I've seen this type of thing on the Animal Channel*, Gabriel felt.

His small size was actually an advantage though, since he was able to wriggle his way through the forest of legs to a reasonable degree, knees to the chin be damned. He wasn't but a few feet into his escape from the melee, when a scrap of food that'd been tossed aside found its way smack-dab onto Gabriel's head, shocking him into stillness. He slowly pulled it from his forehead and inspected it. What it was, he couldn't be sure. An animal part? A confection of some sort? It contained many hues from the rainbow, and in that regard was candy-like, but at the same time seemed to be shaped and constructed of some sort of animal flesh. A knee to the back thrust him forward, and the edible-thing flung from his hand to the ground. *Just as well*, he considered.

At that moment, a loud belch echoed through the valley. A belch so loud that Gabriel felt he could smell the breath of the belcher, though he could tell it was from far away. Then as if a gaggle of geese had been given a signal, belch followed belch, and the whole group of thousands of hungry lunatics belched together, and most unsavory of all, added their own farts to the mix. This time, Gabriel most definitely *did* smell the smells, since they were everywhere at once.

So then the eating began again, and Gabriel returned to backing away from the crush of people encircling the feeding table, holding his nose all the while. It was then that he noticed that everyone was growing—not tall, but wide. Or to put it another way—fat. The food was really flying now, and as he stood there, stunned in amazement, he could see the pounds being put on, inch after flabby inch. Butts got bigger. Arms got thicker.

Feet and ankles became engorged. And when a woman, who only moments earlier had been thin and attractive, looked down at Gabriel in passing curiosity, he beheld the shape-shifted horror of a large, pumpkin-like head of jiggling fat, smiling in glee, juices of food painting her visage like war paint to the battle.

And they didn't stop growing. Like dirigibles readying for flight, they inflated bigger and bigger with each bite, becoming rounder and pimplier, sweating more, getting greasier, and in general, becoming most ridiculously corpulent.

Disgust began to seep into Gabriel's mind, but then a small drop of the slop that'd banged into his head earlier made its way down his left cheek and into the corner of his mouth.

He tasted it.

Beyond all understanding, it was the most wonderful flavor that he'd ever tasted, and also, he was now unbelievably hungry. Gabriel had been hungry before in his short life, certainly, but nothing prepared him for this. His spirit shook with intense desire to eat—to use his jaw like a shark, chewing and ripping to bits anything remotely passing for food—and the best food in all the universe as far as he could tell sat but a few feet away on a table, just beyond his reach.

Much like a deranged cartoon character, Gabriel made for the table, unstoppable. Knees; thighs; who cared? His intense culinary need focused his movement like a kung fu master on a tear, and he dodged every moving limb-obstacle brilliantly. Once at the table, he lunged upward and quickly scaled the back of an unaware, gorging pig-balloon of a human, and plopped himself feet-first onto the food-piled table. Reaching down, he grabbed at the multicolored, flesh-like stuff with both fists, and brought the bizarre sludge up to the precipice of his wide open mouth. It was at this moment that he caught a glimpse of all around him being high up on the table, and he could see from horizon to horizon, fat, bloated, stinking people, their white togas now nothing better than discolored and torn napkins, for their greasy leavings. Moans and groans of intense pleasure filled the valley, but sounded more like moos and bleats, somehow. All in all, it was a disquieting vision, to say the least, and Gabriel thought for a moment. It then hit him square in the brain that should he actually take a bite of this odd but wonderful feast-fodder, he then would be stuck eternally in this level of the underworld, gorging and engorging through time and space the same incredibly wonderful tasting food-stuffs, over and over. *Not much of an existence*, Gabriel considered.

But the more Gabriel pondered this, the more it seemed heavenly, sort of. *I'm really hungry!* Gabriel felt, and decided that there were fates worse than this. With his stomach screaming for sustenance, he opened his mouth wide, he did, and as he pushed the stuff toward his awaiting gullet, he heard a sound that startled him. No mistaking it: just as the burping round earlier began with one single belch, then grew to a cacophony of simultaneous belching, as if on cue, projectile-vomit was now flying forth, as far as the eye could see, from every mouth. Splashing at feet, covering the ground, painting the already dirty togas a brilliant hue of stinking green and yellow, it just kept coming and coming. And as it came wave after wave, the bodies of these poor souls slowly shrank back to their previous healthy sizes. Vomit flung everywhere. Into hair, onto faces, into eyes, and unfortunately for Gabriel, into his hair too. Everything was now, it seemed, coated in a layer of puke, and the stench was unbelievably bad. It was the most heinously, nose-burning foulness ever to cross Gabriel's smell-nerves. And even though Gabriel had yet to eat anything, he began to wretch from the foulness of the whole thing; never mind that his stomach was empty and nothing came forth.

He flung the foul food that only moments earlier he'd hoped to consume from his hands, retching all the while and slid from the edge of the table onto the ground, a shocked and beaten boy-soul. All around him, the deviants were back to gorging from the tables, their stomachs empty and ready for more, but Gabriel was too ill at heart and stomach to notice much anymore. He slowly made his way from the non-stop clamor and mess, not caring nor having the energy to react to the occasional errant knee to the chin or thigh to the shoulder. His involuntary retching decreased in frequency, since the farther away from the center of the madness he trod, the less vomit his feet slipped through. Soon, he saw green, happy grass under his feet, then glanced back and realized that he was leaving the "valley of the gorge" behind. Onward he pushed, not sure what was next, but one thing he did know: he wasn't hungry anymore.

THE INSANE ASYLUM

GABRIEL MADE HIS way through unspoiled green pastures and meadows, happy to be alone again, but slightly unnerved by the omnipresent sunshine. It was nice and warm, but kinda creepy, like hanging out with someone who never stops smiling.

His clothes were a tatter, and smelly too. His hair was dried hard and a bit sticky, the side-effect to it having been barfed on earlier. He was able to gather his wits about him in mental solitude though, and that was good, although he did have a hard time ignoring a small amount of anxiousness—probably inspired by the reasonable assumption that some sort of "thing" was bound to present itself to him, sooner or later, that would confuse, astound and/or terrify him, but not necessarily in that order.

Cresting a hillside, Gabriel noticed at his feet what looked to be the scant beginnings of a well-hewn dirt trail. *Evidence of creatures of some sort. Hopefully pleasant humans*, were Gabriel's thoughts.

Looking up, he realized that the trail wound its way between and over the hills and valleys that lay ahead of him to the distance. Gabriel wondered if to use it was to risk entrapment, but he quickly admonished himself for being paranoid, even though he'd be stupid not to be paranoid, after what he'd been through. Regardless, half out of curiosity, half out of boredom, and half out of not knowing what else to do, he set foot to the trail with confidence, and walk it, he did.

After a fashion, Gabriel hit his stride, and was most happy with his situation. He was setting forth at a nice clip, his surroundings were beautiful, and he'd very nearly forgotten the dried puke that encrusted his body, it having cracked and fallen away to a degree. Through meadow after meadow of low lying hills and valleys, Gabriel trundled forth, receiving energy from the omnipresent sun and absorbing the natural beauty around him. Not only was the sun always shining high in the sky, but it was sunlight of an incredible quality— the type you only rarely see on Earth, after a good rain, when everything sparkles with glee, and your eyes are deliriously happy to soak it all in.

Thought after thought cascaded through Gabriel's mind as it was functioning at a frantic clip. He was only eleven years old, but he was smart and had learned a lot things, and now, for some reason, his brain was making all sorts of interesting connections. His excitement increased exponentially, since his intellect seemed to be growing moment to moment. Gabriel was beginning to have delusions of grandeur too—beginning to think he was another Da Vinci or the like. His mind was building flying contraptions with umbrellas and box fans, cars were running on lemonade, and he was erecting high-rise buildings with bamboo and virtual reality software. It was all so clear!

Amidst a particularly deep creative revelry, Gabriel happened to take quick notice of the fact that the trail ended abruptly, whilst sending his right foot forward. His stomach twisted in fear when he realized that there was no ground beneath it. Instinct kicking into overdrive, he dug his left heel into the soil and managed to torque his body, spinning backwards, falling flat on his face with a most ignominious thud. Da Vinci, indeed! As he lay there, grass and dirt digging themselves between his fat lip and into the spaces between his teeth, he couldn't help but notice the disquieting sensation that his feet were hanging over the edge of something.

Pushing himself up, he turned and sat, spat the bits of ground from his mouth, and realized that his feet were indeed hanging off the edge of something—and in Gabriel's estimation at the moment, it seemed to be the edge of the world.

Gabriel slowly stood and gazed forward. From a point only inches from the toes of his shoes, to what seemed infinity in the distance, the ground gave way to an impossibly huge abyss; gray overcast, foreboding, fog-filled, with skies bursting with roiling and angry clouds. He glanced to his left, then quickly to his right. From both viewpoints, the sharp drop-off went on forever to the horizon, as if the entire planet had been cleaved cleanly at an exact longitude. He sensed a chill in the air.

He turned 180 degrees to survey from whence he came, and the happy, warm, sunshine land greeted him, as before.

He turned back to the abyss, and unable to bridle his curiosity, stepped forward. He gingerly peered over the edge and down into these newly discovered depths.

Vertigo almost pulled him from his feet and over the edge, itself. Miles of distance straight down. Deep, deep, ridiculously deep! And at what Gabriel perceived to be the very bottom, lay a slate grey sea, slowly undulating undercover of translucent fog.

Gabriel was frozen in place by awe over the enormity of the natural wonder he was witnessing. His jaw slacked, and his knees began to buckle ever so slightly, and it was when he sensed himself tipping forward, seemingly pulled by the dark majesty of the gulf, that he jumped backwards, onto safer footing.

It was at this very moment when he felt secure, both feet on firm ground, that he heard the screaming. To his left, far in the distance, came the screech, but accompanied by the Doppler effect. Gabriel had recently learned about the Doppler effect. As a sound got closer and closer, it raised in frequency. Sure enough, the scream's pitch was rising, as was the volume, and

Gabriel turned to inspect what was clearly heading his way, and quite fast.

It was a humanoid of sorts. Hard to make out. Dull, grey skin, and maybe had six or more limbs that worked more like the spokes of a spinning flesh wheel, propelling the odd, apparently unhappy beast at a rapid rate, directly toward the edge of the abyss.

Gabriel watched in horror as the thing flung itself into the vast, empty, gray expanse. It had been running so fast that it seemed to hang in the air for just a bit too long, much like that coyote from his Saturday morning cartoons. And just as Mr. Doppler would have predicted, the pitch of its wail decreased in frequency as it slowly but surely made its way straight down into the cold, awaiting sea. Although the screams eventually drew silent, Gabriel thought he could just make out the sound of a splash, a few moments after he saw the beast disappear into the fog and waves.

Gabriel had but a moment to think, when he heard another battle cry, this time from behind his right ear. And he witnessed the same exact self-sacrifice, although this creature was more giraffe-like, and was riding some sort of rickety bike-like apparatus that was nonetheless propelling him at a nice clip.

Off the edge the giraffe-man went, screaming his lungs out, then disappearing into Gabriel's memory.

Needless to say, Gabriel was taken aback by what he'd just witnessed. He considered going back into Sunshine Land, but was compelled to stay where he was and contemplate the situation more fully. He found a small mound near the rim of the abyss and sat down to think. As he sat there over the next hour or so, having a hard time making heads or tails of the goings on, he was witness to twelve more hapless leaps into the void. Every creature different, but just as intent to go off the cliff as the last.

He saw a human—albeit with green skin and an antenna sticking out the top of its head—do the deed; what seemed to be an overgrown DNA molecule with eyes, (and a mouth!) too. A large cockroach-like thing driving a spoon the size of a small car came next. Such a parade that he stopped taking note of the variety and nearly became bored.

It was then that the idea struck him like a thunderbolt. He was going over, just like the rest! *Why not?* he thought to himself. *I'll get a good wash, which I need desperately, and besides, it looks like fun!*

Gabriel literally could not stop himself. It was as if someone flicked a switch in his soul, and he had no choice but to go. He hadn't even a scintilla of doubt!

He eagerly ran nearly a football field's length back from the cliff's edge, stopped, turned, steadied himself, and then shot forward like a cannon ball, running so fast that he couldn't believe it. He began to shriek in delight. This was the most fun he'd ever had! Better than the Murder Clown Roller Coaster that he'd rode last summer. Actually, much, much better. He felt like he was flying, and in what seemed an instant, he'd cleared the edge. He looked down as gravity's tug slowed him, and he saw the enormous, ominous sea bubbling below, filling his entire view. Slowly, he began falling, and the sea lurched closer and closer as he gained speed. Gabriel was feeling like a missile on a mission. His shrieking was constant as was his glee. He simply couldn't believe his good fortune.

With a splash, he shot into the water, feet first, slicing it like a knife through lard. He felt no pain—more like a rubbery sensation that made him think of jello.

As the bubbles from his splash cleared from his vision, he could make out thousands of creatures through miles of blue-green, crystal clear water, making their way to the bottom of this strange ocean in the same fashion that he was. Happily, breathing wasn't an issue, but Gabriel wasn't surprised. He simply grinned and let the momentum of his fall carry him to the same unknown destination that he and all the others were apparently destined to find.

Looking down between his feet, he could just barely make out a structure of some sort, looking vaguely like the yawning openings of gigantic smokestacks. Gabriel's heart skipped a beat. As he got closer, the structures became clearer, and he was able to see what seemed a whole row of dozens of these things situated firmly at the bottom of a ravine. And as he drew even closer, he realized that he, along with all the others, was actually being sucked into these portals from left to right as far as he could see. Beings were being pulled into these maws in streams, much like a large school of fish being divided into various sewer pipes.

Sewer pipes! Cripes! I'm being sucked into a sewage system! Aaaaahhhh!

But before Gabriel could finish his regretful musings, he was banging into others as his pathway was set, and he was now being pulled into the entrance of one particular gigantic entryway with hundreds of other hapless beings, much like cars being squeezed into the path of a single toll booth.

Fascination took over from fear though, as Gabriel could catch the occasional detailed glimpse of the thing that was pulling him in between the mêlée of body parts that he was now wrestling with. From the exterior, it seemed like something very, very old—like an Egyptian pyramid—with eons of wear and tear, but the further he was pulled into it, it seemed more akin to modern technology, like how Gabriel would imagine the inner workings of a spaceship. And the interior of it pulsed too, almost as if it was the lining of a living organism. And it glowed a bit as well, kinda like a firefly's soft green hue. In fact, when he looked to where he was headed, far off into the murky distance of the giant pipe, a bright, greenish glow seemed to mark everyone's destination. *Don't think this is a sewage pipe after all*, Gabriel concluded.

"Where are you going?" came the query, as a friendly creature overtook Gabriel at his port bow.

"Excuse me?" Gabriel blurted, bubbles marking his words.

"Where are you *going*?" said the two-headed sheep, out of his right head. His left head seemed indifferent and bored.

"Uh…"

"I see…You're not from around here, are you?"

"Well, no I'm not," Gabriel managed.

"Hey, Lug!" the right head turned to its shoulder partner, addressing it. "This guy's not from around here! He has no idea what's up!"

"Whatever," came the dismissive retort.

"I mean," still addressing his other head, "this little kid's lost! Like, totally lost!"

The other head smirked, scratched its left cheek with its hoof, then stuck its tongue out, licked the hoof, and began to smooth over some rough fleece at the crown of his skull. He clearly couldn't have cared less.

"Uh, well, anyway"—the right sheep head turned back to Gabriel—"I don't mean to alarm you, kid, but if you don't know where you're going, or you haven't been given an assignment, you could end up anywhere!"

Gabriel gulped. An air bubble escaped his throat as if to punctuate his sudden onset of fear. The caring sheep-head took notice.

"Gosh! I'm sorry kid! I don't mean to...what's your name again?"

"Gabriel," said Gabriel.

"I don't mean to alarm you, Gabriel. I'm sure you'll be fine. Just make sure that you read the signs carefully before we enter the distribution center."

"Huh?"

"The signs, Gabriel. Just make sure you read the signs before we—"

The nice sheep-head's words were cut off by the rude arrival of what seemed like a large sack of muscle and bone, with grey, scaly skin and three pink eyeballs. It might as well have been a bowling ball, and Gabriel and the two-headed sheep were but pins.

"Outta my way!" it bellowed, as it plowed on through.

The two-headed sheep was quickly bounced aside, and other tumbling creatures filled in his space. Gabriel could see that the friendly half of the double-headed sheep was still attempting to shout something of importance, seemingly, but he simply couldn't hear it, what with the bubbles and general chaos around him, so he thought it better to steel himself for whatever lay ahead further on down the tunnel.

So, Gabriel was but a herded animal, jammed into a floating, watery cacophony of thousands of huddled others, being pulled through what amounted to a gigantic high-tech esophagus, whose interior walls undulated and glowed a soothing green glow. Salmon crowding a narrow steam came to mind. *No matter*, thought Gabriel. *All I can do is just float down stream, so I might as well relax.*

"Wake up!" shot the insistent order, including a punch to the belly for emphasis. Gabriel awoke with a start just in time to see a spinning top bounce off into the crowd. It had angry eyes, somehow, and they were piercing the water between them and Gabriel's eyes, most emphatically. Then it disappeared amongst the floating sentient jetsam.

Apparently, Gabriel'd fallen asleep. Not hard to do whilst drifting along in a warm liquid, aimlessly. But before he could right his mental state, and clear out his cobwebs of thought, a shocking revelation brought him to full attention.

In all directions—above, below, and to the left and right of him—were pink, blinking neon signs, hundreds of them. He was slipping past them fast, like a speeding car on a highway, barely able to read a single one. *Belfinshlicker* he thought he saw. *Nekeldorne* was another. *Zaklephuldenkel?*

And each sign seemed to correspond to an exit from this watery tube. Indeed, Gabriel could see creatures taking these exits in droves, tributaries of beings disappearing into small, black holes that lined the interior of the main trafficway.

In an alarmingly quick fashion, the population that had kept Gabriel company in travel dwindled to the point of panicking him greatly, because clearly, everyone else knew exactly where they were going, and Gabriel had no idea what the heck was going on! And he was in grave danger of being left alone, he feared, since his choice of exits was dwindling to but a few. He realized too that he was reaching the end of the line, , when he spotted something that greeted him with an ever-deepening level of terror.

The liquid that was pulling this highway along at a nautical clip was sifting through what seemed a large mechanical mesh, very nearly a half-mile in width, at the very end of this gigantic tubular highway. And if Gabriel wasn't mistaken, he could see hundreds of creatures stuck in the threads of this mesh, thrashing vainly to be freed, or undulating with the water-flow like a dead fish in a fast-moving creek banging up mercilessly against a rock, seeming for a moment to be alive. End of the line, indeed.

In quick, panicky fashion, Gabriel searched for an exit. At this point, only three exit signs remained. There were still other beings traveling with him, he duly noted, so he didn't feel like a total loser, but he had a feeling that Shangri-La wasn't one of these fine destinations.

In rapid succession: *Gam-Lap-Damerjott, Tumjelli,* and *Hellstein.*

Let's see, Gabriel mused. *Gap-Lap-Damerjott sounds interest—*

In a flash, he flew past, and that option was gone. *Aaack!* Gabriel panicked. Only two left. *No way I'm going to Hellstein!* He decided, and how could you blame him?

As if reading his mind, the current grabbed his little body and trust him toward the exit marked *Tumjelli,* although Gabriel was a little dismayed when he glanced back and realized that, among the last few dozens of beings exiting, he was the only one choosing *Tumjelli.*

He thought he could hear a few snide laughs directed his way as he sped to his exit.

Gulp, he thought, as he was thrust into the small black orifice and flung into an entirely new reality.

Gabriel shot from the tight tube, straight up into the air of this new place, like a spit wad from a straw. His trajectory slowed after a few feet, then he lightly and elegantly set down toward the ground like he was made from airy marshmallows. The whole thing happened so fast that he didn't notice the bizarre fact that he might as well have actually been made from marshmallows, for all the utterly freakish nonsensical hullabaloo that surrounded him as he landed.

For, as he surveyed his surroundings after setting foot, Gabriel was quite taken aback by every single detail that met his eyes, even though his eyes were more like the rear ends of yellow rubber duckies, with three bright-red bike-reflector looking things on each.

He knew this because the ground underfoot was a silken mirror that gave way like a most comfortable pillow with each step, and it reflected all that tread upon it in multitudes of psychedelic fun house colors.

Deeply inspecting this new and twisted visage of himself, Gabriel couldn't help but notice that his head looked as best as could be described as a furry frying pan, with the black plastic handle acting as his neck. His ears were not human ears anymore, but were instead small, disturbing clown faces, grimacing at whatever passed on either side of Gabriel's head, as if they had minds of their own.

His nose set forth from the shallow pan of his face like a toy rocket projecting forward. *It's a toy rocket!* Gabriel decided. *Striped in red and white!*

His mouth looked for all the world like the grill of a heating fixture, not too unlike the one in his bedroom set in the wall near the baseboard.

Looking down at himself, he realized that his torso was constructed with red, blue, and white Legos, or something similar in a random pattern. Below the torso, and acting like a pelvis of sorts, floated a tight collection of eight bowling balls, all seemingly held together like magnets, but not touching. Each ball that Gabriel could see was a different color: a black one, a pearlized blue one, a white and red striped one, as well as other classic bowling ball color schemes. And they all spun slowly, like little planets.

Beneath this, his "legs" protruded down to the ground, but instead of two, there were five of them, and they looked suspiciously like eggbeaters that bent at the knee, the spinning beater being the "foot." In fact, the spinning motion of all five beaters propelled him along as they touch the ground in random succession, giving him the look of a drunken crab as he walked.

Gabriel was most happy to realize though, that his arms and hands were his, the same as they were the day he first set foot on this unthinkable journey. This fact comforted him a bit, and he found himself staring at his hands instinctively in an attempt to relax.

A moment later, Gabriel looked up and took in his surroundings in more detail. He seemed to be walking in the midst of a bustling city square, surrounded by the most inexplicable creatures he'd ever seen. And everywhere were impossible buildings shaped from things common and never before conceived, and fantastical ribbon-like roads, twisting up into the sky, then burrowing deep down into the ground.

Floating items filled the sky. Right above him, for instance, was a transparent, but huge robot-like face that filled half his view and seemed to be laughing at all below its gaze.

Balloons in all shapes, colors, and sizes where everywhere, to the end of the horizon it seemed, as were large, inflated versions of just about every household item one could think of: screwdrivers, armchairs, remote controls, you name it. But there was something odd about each one, other than the fact that they were big, and drifting everywhere. The screwdriver, for instance, had gorilla-like arms that hung limply from its handle, and the armchair was upside down, with the yoke of a Giganotosaurus egg setting firmly upon its top, acting like a brooding, mustard-colored eye.

To his left Gabriel spied the largest building in the square, and it looked for the life of him to be the ribcage of an enormous creature, with windows lining each rib, and each rib interconnected to the other ribs by all sorts of twisted walkways and slides, with creatures streaming up and down them back and forth, like ants to ice cream. At the top of the ribcage where the head should have been sat a large blue and orange globe that spun swiftly and bounced up and down randomly. It made no sense, but Gabriel understood somehow that this was the town clock.

To his right, Gabriel's eyes partook of a clownish feast of buildings fashioned to look like gigantic, upside-down carrots, with their leafy "tops" providing the base of each tower, and with each carrot sprouting windows in random placement, much like the overgrown roots of a normal carrot. And the carrot towers weren't all orange, either. One of them was, but the others were all different—from purple, to mint green, to royal blue, and shining, brilliant gold.

Across the street from that conflagration of an oddity sat a yellow sponge of a building, with each wet, spongy hole eagerly sucking into itself any passersby that got close enough. Where they ended up after entering the building was anyone's guess, and Gabriel wasn't too eager to find out.

"Bunga jig-na-leggings?"

"Hunkle-deng?" came Gabriel's reply, although he was quite sure that he'd just said "Excuse me?"

Facing Gabriel directly was a white paper cup the size of a man with spider legs and simple, cartoonish facial features painted onto the cup with thick red paint. Looking hand-animated, the painted features moved as it spoke.

"Bunga jig-na-leggings?" it implored again, although suddenly, Gabriel could understand the language. The paper cup was asking Gabriel if he was "new here."

"Nal bebba do-doon," was Gabriel's reply. Or rather, "Yes."

"Ga nefavuh nel melak a denk devuld, guzza weev a mer tennel frop. Goozy Wenk dip nu vuld, grink a mer stunch Geven." The paper cup explained.

In Gabriel's mind this vocalization came across as: *I would suggest, then, that you go to the "Pigeon Palace" at Eighty-Third and Cross Street, since they know how to show a guy a good time!* The paper cup then smiled wider than Gabriel thought it possible for any mouth to smile. It must've had a hundred teeth, for one.

Gabriel got a creepy feeling.

"Mert duva dook le meklen duve"

Thanks but no thanks, was what he'd said.

The paper cup then frowned a frown bigger than any Gabriel'd ever seen, and in a flash disappeared into the ground, like a trap door had flung open and sucked him under. Gabriel was quite relieved.

Seeing a sign in the distance for the Pigeon Palace (or rather as Gabriel saw it, *Goozy Wenk*), Gabriel promptly turned 180 degrees and headed in the exact opposite direction. He had no idea where he was going, but it seemed as good a notion as any.

Ambling as he was across the reflective blanket that was the ground, moving not fast at all, but sure—even though you might think otherwise if you saw his strange, tangled gait—Gabriel couldn't help but think how bizarrely different this leisurely walk was from the one he'd had not too long ago, over rolling green fields and under eternally shining sun.

And just as that place had influenced Gabriel's thoughts, this new place was beginning to do the same as well. For as his five eggbeater legs pushed forward, his feet spinning into the ground with each step propelling him forward, Gabriel began to think that "cows" were "never," that "purple" was a "dog," and that "cold" was a building that stood three feet high and held "slippery" in its basement (which was also a canister of beveled).

Gabriel rubbed his ducktail eyes, trying to rid himself of his confusion. He stared out into space to find something solid for his brain to latch onto, but the strange creature that was passing him on his left was not actually the fir tree with tank treads for feet and a cow skull for a head that it appeared to be, but rather an energy being of some kind with vortices emanating forth in all sorts of psychedelic fashions, twisting space and time into something that resembled a dancing DNA molecule made from a billion grape-tasting, electrically charged Egyptian pyramids.

And just when he thought he had a handle on that, another creature appeared—an antique writing desk with rotary pay phones for feet, small jet engines for arms, and a large, purple, eight-lobed throbbing brain for a head—and it suddenly showed its true self, which was a stick figure, just like from a hangman game. At least for a moment it was. And then it wasn't. Now it was something else. It was a vortex that was pulling Gabriel into its twisting center. He couldn't help it. He leaned in, face first. And then he was…five feet from where he'd been a moment earlier, still in the city square. He paused, thought strange thoughts for a moment (like "six" is composed of millions of "drizzle"), and then turned back and saw the throbbing-brain writing desk clunk away on its pay phone feet, and also the fir tree with tank treads forging onward, as if nothing strange had just transpired. *Most odd*, thought Gabriel. *Although* odd *controls* frequency, *and* thought *equals* pie, *and, well…*

"Bekter wankle ne gaaad!" came the interruption. *Snap out of it*, was what it meant.

Gabriel looked up, startled, his panhandle neck creaking at the strain. Bounding toward him like a giant orange boot rolling down a hill was, well, a giant orange boot, tumbling through the square at great insistence. It came to a sudden stop right next to Gabriel, sole of the boot properly flat to the ground with a thud, and four little ceramic angels appeared beneath, raising the boot at all four corners like little, fragile cherubim legs.

"Bekter wankle ne gaaad!" it said again. "Cran lafta noodle narg!" (You're losing it, pal!)

Gabriel couldn't discern where the voice was coming from as the boot seemed to have no face, so he implored, "Hunkle-deng?" (Excuse me?)

"Murt ta leble wen" came the reply., or rather, *Over here, pal!*

Gabriel followed the voice to the side of the shoe, and there saw a large, cartoon sheep head, that had been printed onto the side. He recognized it.

"Dar lepta nek ta boon!" said the two-dimensional, cartoon sheep head. *That's right, it's me!*

"Septun yun mega laf tinkle rane. Alluh nun fir tembu lemmel dift er. Wast res ger tungluh jert, Gabriel?" Or, translated, *We met in the Trammel Slosh Tube, remember? I was wondering where you'd end up! Your name's Gabriel, right?*

"Burzel" was Gabriel's affirmative reply. And just for laughs, Gabriel walked around the boot to the other side, and sure enough, there was the other sheep head. *I believe* Lug *is his name?* Gabriel thought. And Lug's countenance was just as Gabriel remembered: totally, absolutely, completely, and irrevocably disinterested in him. Only after Gabriel stared at Lug for an uncomfortably long period of time—seeing no reaction at all—

did one cartoon eye of Lug's finally, ever so slowly, turn Gabriel's way, with upper eyelid at half-mast for disinterested effect. After a moment, then, Lug smacked his lips as if to underscore his complete disregard. Wise to Lug's game, Gabriel walked back around the big orange boot and addressed the nicer sheep head.

"What's your name?" was Gabriel's question.

"Wig," replied Wig.

"Listen, Gabriel...I'm sorry about Lug. He just can't be bothered for some reason. He's really not that bad of a guy, if you get to know him. I should know, you know?"

"I would think so," Gabriel replied.

"Yeah...He's a-okay. Just a little unfriendly at times, but a-okay."

"So," Wig continued. "How're you doing? You find your way around all right in this crazy place?"

"Where 'am' I?" Gabriel implored, his hot breath scraping past the grill of his mouth. The two then set stride together, the big orange boot being propelled forward with its little angels and their petite, gold, hummingbird-fast wings.

"That's not an easy question to answer," Wig replied. "The best I can come up with is, we're on some sort of interdimensional odyssey, each with our own path to take and lessons to learn. I've been bouncing around here for many years, and I keep thinking that I'm getting somewhere, but I keep going in circles."

"Where else have you been?" Gabriel inquired. At this, Lug smacked his lips even louder than before, to make his displeasure known about something.

"Well," Wig continued, clearing his throat. "'We've' been to Vomitus, Capernicum, Zentopia, and, well…'here.'"

"What's this place called? Tumjell? Jelltum?"

"Tumjelli, I believe, but I…uhh…we call it the Insane Asylum, as nothing here makes sense, and everything is confusing."

"What were you before you arrived in the Underworld? A two-headed sheep?"

"Jeez, I don't know anymore, it's been so long."

"A human!" shouted Lug, angrily, and with little patience. His sudden entrée into the conversation shocked both Wig and Gabriel.

"So was I!" Gabriel added, excitedly.

"Big whoop," was Lug's response to that, which quelled Gabriel's excitement instantly. Lug was good at stuff like that. Wig interjected:

"Well…A human, then, I guess. Lug is almost always right about things like this."

Gabriel regained a bit of his excitement. "Did you come from Earth?" he added.

"OF COURSE!" groaned Lug, in disbelief. And somehow, Gabriel knew it was the last thing he'd hear from Lug, for a long while.

"Um…Well…Anyway…" Wig added apologetically, and then the "two" walked on in silence for a bit. Then:

"Getting back to your original question," Gabriel addressed Wig. "I don't know where I'm going, or how to get there, but I do know that I'm going somewhere, because I've been lots of places already, and I seem to keep moving forward."

"Really?" Wig replied. "Where else have you been?"

"Well, I've been to Hell…"

"OH MY GOD!" shouted Wig. "You've been to Hell? How the hell'd you get out?"

"It's a long story," Gabriel commented, a bit sadly, not wanting to recount much, if anything.

"I bet it is!" came Wig's reply. Lug yawned, loudly.

"And I've been to this place where everybody's really sad and depressed, and—"

"That would be Saq, probably," said Wig. "I haven't been there, but I've heard of it."

Gabriel continued, "and I've been to…wait a second. Where is that other place that you've been? Zen-Land?"

"Zentopia," Wig corrected.

"I haven't been there, yet."

"And you don't wanna go!" Wig countered. "It's a real dead end. That's as far as I've ever gone, and I always get flung right back to where I started. Always. Most infuriating. Besides, it's very dull. There's literally nothing there. And no one to keep you company. It's extremely boring."

"Is it the next level up?" Gabriel was getting excited.

"Gabriel…I'm telling you…You don't want to go there. It's a waste of time and effort."

"You don't understand. I need to find my way back home. I need to get to the next level!"

"That's what everybody wants, Gabriel, but the fact is, you'll probably be stuck down here for eternity, just like most of us."

Gabriel's countenance noticeably saddened.

"But, if you really want to, I can show you how to get there, but it won't—"

"Let's go now!" came Gabriel's curt, but excited reply.

"Okay, then," Wig agreed. He looked around at all of the surreal circus-like confusion that surrounded them, picked a direction, and boldly stated: "That way!"

But just as his big orange boot was turning in the proper direction to lead the way, the Paper Cup with the creepy painted smile and the spindly black spider legs popped up from under foot and blocked Gabriel's turn. And another creature, looking for the world like a bear-sized gas mask with red glowing eyes mounted up on a wheelchair appeared too, and using a long, wood-like contraption that was spring-loaded, sent the doubled-headed orange shoe flying high into the sky, and well enough away for Gabriel to know that he wasn't returning anytime soon, if at all.

The Paper Cup spoke: "No need to bother wasting your time hanging out with that chump. We're going to take you to the Pigeon Palace, just like I offered earlier. My offers are not often turned down. I would advise that you relax, and let us treat you to a good time!"

Gabriel looked over at the glaring red eyes of the gas mask on wheels, and knew in his gut that he had no choice. These two creeps were not to be trifled with, he felt, so Gabriel kept his mouth shut.

"I'll take your silence as a yes. Most excellent!"

So, Paper Cup Man set forth upon his scrawny spider legs, and Gabriel was pushed from behind by the Big Rolling Gas Mask to keep up. Something about this turn of events felt uncomfortably familiar, and Gabriel understood that it wasn't a good thing. Not a good thing at all.

THE PIGEON PALACE

LUGWIG HIT THE dirt with a thud, but righted himself immediately, his angels absorbing the impact like anti-gravity pistons.

He was sorta nowhere, apparently miles from where he'd been while chatting away with Gabriel. It was kinda dusty and empty and a little dark here, like the moment before a big thunderstorm. Wig started:

"I don't wanna hear it."

"Well, you're gunna!" came Lug's retort. "I knew that kid was trouble from the moment I saw him."

"You did not! How can you 'know' a kid is trouble? That makes no sense."

"I just did, is all. And I was right."

"Well…" Wig conceded. "At least I try to help people once in a while. Instead of ignoring everybody else…Right, Lug?"

Lug grumbled in concession, as well.

"I feel bad for that kid," said Wig. "I didn't like those guys at all. Talk about sensing trouble. They're up to no good if you ask me."

"It's not our concern!" added Lug.

"I guess you're right," was Wig's plaintive reply. He suddenly became extremely alarmed. "You don't think that they're taking him to the Pigeon Palace, do you?"

"Of course not. He's just a kid. Relax!"

After a few moments of awkward silence, Wig asked, "Where to now?"

"Your guess is as good as mine," was Lug's useless advice, and they set about moving forth in no particular direction.

Gabriel, all egg-beater-legged, pan-headed, duck-butt-eyed, Lego-bodied bits of him, was in the middle of a caravan of three, with no choice seemingly but to keep up with his new "friends." All around him was the cacophony of this bizarre place called *Tumjelli*—or, as LugWig put it, the Insane Asylum—so there was plenty to keep his eyes and mind occupied on the way to the Pigeon Palace, whatever that was, but still, his heart, whatever it was made of at the moment, was slowly but surely filling with dread.

His dread was being fueled by subtle cues in his surroundings, such as the ominous red glow that clung to the horizon—like a small a-bomb had just detonated there—and how this seemed to be exactly where they were headed; and how the sky above this eerie glow was dark and nasty looking; and how, the closer they got, the fewer goofy oddballs they passed, while at the same time darker, scarier versions of these impossibly odd beings seemed to appear in their stead, as if the whole vibe of the place was shifting gears into something quite unsavory.

Gabriel had a sudden, frightful realization. *I know who these two beings are*, he thought to himself. *It's Payne and Mabel!*

"Right you are, young one!" Payne shrieked as he turned and stared down his quarry. For just a flash of a moment, Payne's evil, disturbed vision appeared in the place of the paper cup, then just as quickly disappeared. Gabriel turned sharply to see if Mabel was bringing up the rear, and sure enough for a split second, the gas mask shone itself to be an angry, growling dog's snout. It snapped at Gabriel for good measure, before disappearing.

"Most excellent! Most excellent!" Trumpeted Payne, now faced forward to the lead.

"Good to have you back, my dear boy. And to think that you almost got away. No one's ever gotten away from Mabel and I… Never! Our perfect streak will continue on. Satan will be most pleased."

"This isn't fair! Satan himself sent me out of Hell. He told me I didn't belong there! He's gunna be pissed at you. This isn't fair!"

"My dear boy," Payne counseled in soothing, even tones, "first of all, Satan will not be pissed. He'll be most pleased, because the more condemned souls he controls, the better, as far as he's concerned. Also, who cares about 'fair'? Fair? Hahaha! There is no such thing, and there never has been, and the sooner you get used to that, the better. Besides, you read the fine print on the certificate, I'm quite sure. Once you return, you can never leave again! It won't matter what Satan thinks! Hahahahaha!"

Panicked, Gabriel made an adrenalin-fueled dash for it, but only managed to get three or four inches away, because instantly, bars of iridescent, multi-hued energy shot forth from Mabel's wheelchair, and encased Gabriel from all sides—top and bottom—in a cage. And for good measure, Gabriel watched glumly as a thin, rope-like strand of energy weaved its way in and out of the beater tangs of his feet and pulled itself taut and knotted, rendering his legs useless. He was now officially helpless and being carted off to his horrid destination.

"Relax, Gabriel, relax. The way I look at it, whether it was a mistake or not, the fact that you ended up in hell in the first place means that you deserve to be there, regardless. Haven't you considered that?"

"But I'm not in hell anymore," Gabriel countered listlessly, with a fatalistic tone of defeat.

Payne countered: "There's no getting away from demons like Mabel and I, I'm afraid. We have full reign throughout the underworld, my boy, and spend our time traveling these realms, causing pain and anguish wherever we go. Boy, do I love my job!"

"Good for you," Gabriel mustered, with an appropriate amount of heartbroken sarcasm.

"Don't be so glum. We're almost there! See."

Gabriel looked up and beheld what could only have been the Pigeon Palace, since it was quite a large castle, the main body of which seemed carved or built from a gargantuan pigeon carcass. And smaller sections of the castle, like the towers and side-structures, were formed from smaller pigeons. Everything was made from pigeons, in fact, whatever their size. And not happy, healthy pigeons, either, but morose, decaying pigeons. Oddly though, the beaks and eyes of every pigeon wore makeup with messy amounts of fluorescent red and blue lipstick and eye-shadow, making each deathly pigeon look, at least at first glance, strangely inviting. The effect was disquieting, to say the least.

As they approached the entrance to the place, beings of all odd stripes stepped aside with quick, fear-filled steps, making way for the three of them. A murmur was sent loose in the crowd as the dark power of Payne and Mabel was sensed by the throng, and Gabriel felt like a prisoner being taken to gallows, inexorably.

"Ah! Here we are, then," Payne remarked. Mabel happily barked in reply.

They stopped for a moment to savor the scene, and Gabriel got a good look at the entrance to the Pigeon Palace. It was, for all he could tell, a red, throbbing orifice that seemed to wend its way downward into the ground. A bluish, translucent cloud of energy undulated across its pink, fleshy folds, as if to invite the traveler inside. It was, Gabriel had no doubt, a portal straight back to hell.

"Right again, my boy! You're always on top of things, that's for sure." Payne prodded. "Maybe Satan can put your smarts to good use. Or maybe he'll just eat your brains!"

Mabel barked her approval.

"Shall we?" Payne invited, one spidery leg extended in polite gesture. Mabel barked once more, and the caravan lurched forward, with only inches to go until they re-entered hell. Gabriel braced for the worst.

Out of the sky shot the large, orange tennis shoe, swooping down like a jet fighter, its little angels acting more like jet engines. Before Payne and Mabel knew what hit them, the angels brought forth a bright yellow energy beam that cascaded down from the sky and destroyed the sinister energy cage that was keeping Gabriel captive; at the same time, they sent a rope-like appendage that grabbed a stunned Gabriel about the waist and hoisted him instantly into the back of the shoe. The shoe, Gabriel in tow, then shot high up into the sky.

It then stopped on a dime, tilted downward, and fired from its opening with deadly aim a bright, lime-green energy ball that made a direct hit into the entrance of the Pigeon Palace. As it ripped through the orifice and through space and time, it grabbed all around it in a temporal web—including Payne and Mabel—and pulled them underneath, as it sheared into the ground.

Gabriel swore he heard Payne shouting "You haven't heard the last of me, my boy!" an instant before he and Mabel disappeared beneath the waves of temporal disturbance. A moment later, a charge exploded, heaving the Pigeon Palace and the grounds that it sat upon upwards, like a humongous belch of a belly. The Palace and the earth around it cracked to brittle bits and slowly, and with much gravity, fell down into the newly made subterranean crater, like swill going down a drain.

"We have to get out of here quickly!" Wig urged. "Those bastards got what they deserved, but it's not exactly kosher to go chucking continuum-busting bombs around, willy-nilly. The authorities will be after us, soon."

"Yes they will!" grumbled Lug.

"Thanks, guys," was all Gabriel could add.

No one was in the mood to talk any further, though. Gabriel was attached safely to the back of the shoe, and that's all he cared about, as a wave of happy exhaustion overtook him to thankful sleep.

ZENTOPIA

LUG AND WIG'S loud, fearful shrieking awoke Gabriel with a start, as did also the waves of intense heat that were blasting by his head in rapid succession, much too close for comfort. Gabriel understood instantly that they were being fired upon by "the authorities," and he glanced back to confirm this fact, just in time to witness an energy torpedo miss his hairy pan-head by a few centimeters. It had been fired through the nostril of an oversized, jet-propelled, hot-pink sunglasses and goofy-nose combination, just like the Groucho glasses Gabriel'd seen online. And there were five of these things firing away, and they were gaining ground. Gabriel turned forward and clung tightly to the back of the shoe, not laughing at all.

"We're almost there!" shrieked Wig.

"We'll never make it!" Lug shrieked in return.

"We're almost there! We can make it! We can make it!"

"This is all your fault!" Lug yelled.

"Oh, cram it to hell!" Wig yelled back.

Gabriel took a peek forward and glanced at their destination.

On a mustard-colored plain—covered for miles with craters of various depths and widths—sat a dark, lonely, wooden doorway, and LugWig, with Gabriel attached, were headed straight for it, like a missile.

Gabriel noticed too, that the pursuers had seemingly changed their strategy, and were now trying to destroy the portal, instead of them, with shot after shot just missing the doorway, encircling it with ever more craters.

Flying at jet speed, Gabriel knew this would all be over in a scant few seconds, and indeed it was, since the sunglasses turned skyward, giving up chase, not wanting to slam into the ground, and the innocuous little wooden doorway, suddenly much bigger, opened its door in a welcoming gesture, as the new arrivals passed through it, like a bowling ball shot through water.

On the other side, LugWig and Gabriel popped into existence like a switch had been flicked, appearing none the worse for wear, and back to their "normal" selves, feet planted firmly on the ground. Gabriel gave himself a once over and realized quite quickly that he was in human form again. He glanced over at LugWig and saw that he was as when he first met him: a two-headed sheep. *What an odd creature*, thought Gabriel. He then partook of his surroundings and realized that he seemed to be, for lack of a better phrase, absolutely nowhere. As far as could be seen, in all directions, was nothing but flat horizon, and there was no color to be had, either, but for the light blues in Gabriel's clothing, his pale peach complexion, and the dark, eggplant purple of LugWig's two sheep faces. Everything else though was a bland grayish white. The ground, the sky, the air: they all melted into each other, creating a vast sense of bland. There was, however, a slight sound of wind in the far distance, but that only punctuated the sense of intense loneliness and isolation that was already overtaking Gabriel's soul.

"I told you it was really boring here, kid!" Wig offered, as he rubbed his watery eyes with his front leg—preening, cleaning, and licking. Wig put his foot back down, then Lug raised his, and preened in the same animal fashion.

"No more odd words," Gabriel noted.

"Oh no," continued Wig. "Normal language again…"

"So this is Zentopia?" asked Gabriel.

"I'm afraid so," said Wig

"Why didn't they follow us here?" Gabriel queried.

"It's not their jurisdiction, sorta. You understand?"

"I think so," he admitted.

"It's not their business anymore. They will, no doubt, alert the authorities on this plane, but if my experience is any indication, we won't be bothered here. There's not a lot of cooperation between the two realms, you know?"

"I see..."

"You *know* that you and I are stuck here, Wig!" shot Lug, quite angry.

"No, we're not!" Wig countered.

"Yes, we are!" Lug continued, grumbling noticeably. "Every time we've ended up here, we're always sent back to lower realms instead of advancing to the next plane, and we always get sent through the Insane Asylum when we're making our way back up, no matter what exits we take in the Trammel Slosh Tube. Now that we're wanted in the Insane Asylum, we can't leave here, because we'll end up there! We're stuck here forever."

Wig suddenly went glum. It was hard to argue Lug's logic, but Lug *always* saw the dark side, and Wig always saw the bright, so he cheered up quickly and added: "We'll figure something out. We always do."

"You and that stupid kid!" Lug twisted the knife a bit more. "What's so freakin' special about this stupid kid that we gotta risk our soul?"

Gabriel suddenly felt extremely guilty, and so did Wig, but he offered this: "I don't know. There's just something about him. I just know that we we're supposed to protect him, is all. Call it instinct."

Gabriel looked Wig in the eyes and suddenly felt a lot better.

"Well, your instincts almost got us killed, or sent to hell, or who knows what!" Lug's tone trailed off a bit as he added: "Anyway..."

For an instant, Gabriel caught a glimpse of Lug's eyes, but Lug turned his head quickly and resolutely, and harrumphed louder than any harrumph Gabriel'd ever heard.

A glum silence filled the space between them, and after a moment or two, LugWig started walking. Gabriel assumed that LugWig knew where he was going, so he followed close behind, in total silence. Silence seemed a fitting tribute to this very empty place, anyway.

Soon, the clip-clop of LugWig's hooves melded with Gabriel's footfalls and created a rhythmic drone that hypnotized him a little. He watched the featureless ground go by beneath his feet, and it set his mind to thinking.

He thought of Emma and how upset she must now be to have accidentally killed her big brother. He thought of his mom and how devastating his death must have been for her. And he thought of his father and how hurtful it was to Gabriel that he was taken from him, when he was but a little kid. It bothered Gabriel deeply that he never got to know his father, since it can't have been a good thing to not have a father, he felt.

Wig spoke up, and it snapped Gabriel out of his reverie: "In case you're wondering, we're headed toward the Temple."

"The *Temple*?" Gabriel asked.

"Yeah," Wig continued. "It's the only thing we've ever found here, and we've been there many times. The

Temple always sends us back to square one though, but maybe you'll have better luck."

Great! Gabriel grumbled to himself. *More portals! I'm sick of portals, and I'm sick of this place! I just want to go home.*

Regardless of Gabriel's wishes, however, he had no choice but to carry on and to trust LugWig as his guide. It did seem odd to Gabriel that LugWig seemed to be both his closest friend, and his most vocal opponent, all wrapped up into one, but Gabriel sensed ultimately that LugWig was a good-hearted sort—warts and all—and that he would help Gabriel as best he could to find his way.

So, the two (or should I say, three) of them walked on in silence, keeping to themselves. The grayness that surrounded them never lifted or shifted, and it seeped into their very souls, distilling in them an inability to sense or understand anything but the deep core of themselves. There were no distractions of any kind, save each other, and Gabriel was pulled into unavoidable, uncomfortable self-reflection. It then dawned on him that this was the point of this place: to force you to know yourself, whether you liked it or not. One thing was becoming crystal clear to Gabriel—he wasn't liking it.

For instance, Gabriel was finding it impossible not to conclude that he was a very self-important person, indeed, and if it weren't for his own overly-inflated ego, he'd have taken the time to talk to Emma about her new toy—whatever it was—first thing, and she wouldn't have been so desperate to show it to him later, while he was bathing. In a way, his sense of being "better than" Emma brought about his own demise. *What a depressing thought*, Gabriel conceded.

And also, Gabriel's desire to prove to the rest of the world what he perceived to be his great intellect, by studying and reading all that he could—while laudable—was keeping him isolated from other kids, since Gabriel's only real friends were his books. The more he thought about it, the more he realized that he had no friends. No friends! *How pitiful.* Gabriel felt.

And, also…

"There it is!" alerted Wig.

Gabriel started upright and beheld in the distance what looked for the world to be nothing more than an old maple tree, green leaves and all.

"That's it?" was Gabriel's concern.

"Yep! That's it…" replied Wig. "The Temple."

"Doesn't look like a temple to me," countered Gabriel.

"You'll understand when you take a closer look," said Wig.

Gabriel shrugged and started off toward the tree. It only took him a few moments to realize, however, that LugWig wasn't going with him.

Gabriel turned back and queried in a worried tone, "Aren't you coming?"

LugWig, standing resolutely where he'd stopped but a moment earlier, replied through Wig's mouth: "Nope. This is your trip, Gabriel. I've been here before, and I know what'll happen to me. Clearly, you have to face your destiny alone."

Gabriel gulped. "But…"

"No buts about it!" Lug shouted, quite angry. Gabriel jumped straight up a few inches from the shock of Lug's angry explosion.

"I'm afraid it's true," Wig counseled, in friendlier tones. "We've taken you as far as we can. The rest is up to you, now."

Gabriel thought about how he'd come most of his journey alone, anyway, and then calmed down a bit, but there was no doubt in his mind that he'd grown used to LugWig's presence, and he was now more than a little scared.

"I understand..." Gabriel offered, feebly.

"Don't worry about it, kid. It's going to be all right. Now get going, okay?" Wig wiped something from his eye with his forelimb. Gabriel wondered if it was a tear. Lug turned his head to the side, offering a cold shoulder.

"Okay..." Gabriel croaked again. He turned on his heels and walked a few steps in the direction of the tree, but then quickly turned back around. LugWig was still planted like a rock—hadn't moved an inch—and Gabriel knew in his heart with certainty that LugWig would not follow, so he turned back toward the tree one last time and made straight for it.

"What do you think's going to happen to the kid?" Wig asked Lug, after a few long moments of silence.

"Who cares!" was Lug's heartless reply. "I'm more worried about us!"

Disgusted, Wig lifted his forelimb and smacked Lug across the sensitive spot on top his snout.

"HEY!" Lug shouted, and instinctively lifted his forelimb to strike in retaliation. Since LugWig had but two forelimbs, and both were in the air, his body fell to the ground with a thud. A melee ensued with Lug and Wig trading swipes at each other's sheep-heads, twisting and jerking violently in a cloud of grey dust. This wasn't the first time they'd squared off, it seemed.

Gabriel was too far ahead to hear the commotion though, and he kept pushing on to the tree, determined to prove to LugWig that he could handle this like a man. The tree loomed larger and larger in Gabriel's view, the closer he got.

THE TEMPLE

FROM A DISTANCE it seemed but an average tree, but in fact, the Temple was actually quite large. By the time Gabriel had reached its roots, its trunk stood thick and sturdy, the size of a redwood's, and its foliage arched high above Gabriel's head, not unlike a cathedral's awe-inspiring ceiling.

The bark of the tree wasn't normal, natural bark, either, but had a metallic sheen like cast bronze, every square inch of its surface populated with all sorts of interesting symbols and shapes that undulated slowly, as if flesh being pushed and pulled by a dense hive of crawling, subsurface creatures.

Faces—both happy and distressed—morphed into religious symbols, and then back again: yin/yang, crosses of all types, and even the Star of David. But most of the symbols he saw were unrecognizable. Human body parts and curious animals—some familiar, some clearly alien—were also appearing and disappearing, becoming strange things too odd to understand.

In the midst of this confused, living sculpture, sat one symbol that didn't change at all, at Gabriel's eye level. It was round, had an ornate square inscribed in it—corners to circle's edge—and it glowed with a slight, bluish tinge. Gabriel knew it was to be touched for entry, and so he did this, and thus was Gabriel immediately drawn though the wall of the temple like water through a sieve, seeing and feeling every molecule as he went. He was deposited safely inside, tingling a bit from head to toe.

Inside, the temple glowed a warm, inviting orange hue. The walls inside were round as Gabriel had expected—as if the tree had been hollowed out—and Gabriel looked up to see a bright, yellowish light cast down upon the whole affair from the top of the cored-out trunk, painting everything with its bright, golden tones.

Gabriel felt a reverence for this light. It seemed soulful and caring—if a light source could be such a thing—and Gabriel's worries immediately melted away.

He looked down at his feet and beheld a beautiful mandala on the floor, throbbing with life and shifting forms, looking very much like a visage from a kaleidoscope's lens. Its multicolored shapes undulated in a slow, hypnotic rhythm that lulled Gabriel into a meditative state.

His internal soliloquy always active since he could remember, Gabriel's mind was now suddenly stilled and peaceful, and every muscle, bone and tendon of his small frame felt as if it had been freed from a suit of anxiety-forged armor. Gabriel was truly at peace, or so it did seem to him.

In the midst of this reverie, Gabriel saw—growing from the center of the mandala—a bulbous form that slowly morphed into a chair of sorts. It was more like a large, bluish hand, actually, with the palm as the seat, open and inviting, and the fingers tight together and upright, to provide comfortable back support. There was an eye in the middle of the palm, and it blinked at Gabriel.

"Please sit," the chair said.

Feeling no fear and thus no reason to resist, Gabriel did just that and slowly sat down into the palm. The chair then molded itself around Gabriel's back and sides into a perfect fit—the most comfortable seating arrangement Gabriel'd ever had, by far.

Automatically, and without the slightest bit of prompting from his own mind, Gabriel's body pushed and pulled itself into a classic, leg-folded yoga pose. Gabriel looked down at his legs, entwined like pretzels, and was impressed that he could do such a thing.

Again, without thought, his hands twisted and turned themselves into various positions, the likes of which Gabriel had seen Asian dancers use. *Mudras*, is what he remembered these hand positions being called.

After a few moments, he settled down with his right hand up, facing out, and his left hand down, palm out.

And nary a moment later, the world around him—the temple, everything—faded away, and Gabriel found himself floating in a soothing, light blue space, which Gabriel sensed extended infinitely in all directions.

Gabriel wasn't sure how he knew it, but he knew that he wasn't thinking. His mind was perfectly still. And yet, he still had awareness of himself and his surroundings; he simply wasn't thinking about them, or anything else for that matter. It was as if his sense of himself was as a pure musical tone that satisfied his soul, but held no judgment.

It was at this point that a brilliant-hued purple light grew from Gabriel's forehead, and it fanned out from his third eye like a tree sprouting life in all directions. Once covering Gabriel's field of vision, it stopped and steadied itself, and then began to show Gabriel moving images that displayed in vivid detail the very nature of the universe.

There is no beginning came a narrator's voice from deep inside Gabriel's head. *Only birth and rebirth, unending.*

With this, Gabriel witnessed, in unbelievably breathtaking detail, the singularity that began the current universe and that spread in microseconds into all the known—and unknown—forces and building blocks of matter.

He saw a unified force that seemed to him to be but the eye of God split into magnetic and gravitational forces.

He saw matter form from nothing and coalesce into the fundamental substances that formed the universe.

He saw galaxies form star by star and begin to swirl around their black hole cores, pulled through space and time by immense gravitational pull.

He saw planets—millions of them—form from gas and rock and witnessed the formation of life on a large percentage of these planetary bodies.

He saw single-celled life-forms begin and then evolve both slowly and sporadically into larger life-forms of all ridiculous shapes and sizes—some recognizable, but most not.

He saw many an intelligent species on par with humans, in all sorts of different shapes and sizes, with cities and cultures and space travel, and many sentient creatures much, much further evolved than humans. So far ahead, in fact, that they'd be unrecognizable by the comparatively puny human mind.

He saw...

Payne and Mabel?

Their sudden and dramatic entry into Gabriel's deep spiritual reverie registered in Gabriel's brain, and yet he felt no fear whatsoever. The two demons stood there, side by side, filling Gabriel's view entirely, and doing their best to break Gabriel's meditative peace by creating as much chaos as possible.

Dressed as Gabriel originally met him, as the elegant hipster, Payne was screaming at the top of his lungs, all nature of profanity, and yet Gabriel didn't hear a single word. It felt from Gabriel's point of view as if there was an impregnable force field protecting him.

Mabel was yelping, barking, and leaping, and showing as much fang as possible, but this pointless show of force meant nothing to Gabriel. Payne and Mabel quickly realized that they were having no effect, so they redoubled their efforts.

Payne shed his classy human artifice and became his true self: a disgusting, skinless, non-human demon. Mabel shed her illusion of being a dog, as well, and presented herself as a scorched, flaming hellhound, still on all fours, but definitely not a dog anymore. They both tore at the space that divided them from Gabriel, with fangs and nails and insanely intense hatred, and although their combined force seemed to be able to bend the protective seal, it would not break.

And still, not a flinch from Gabriel. He was still floating in utter peace, but watching a bizarre, pointless movie, for all that it meant to him at the moment.

Very chagrinned, but feeling up to the challenge, with a flourishing bodily gesture, Payne filled the entire space behind, above and around the three of them with all the chaos that he could dredge up from hell—all the tormented, disfigured demons; all the tortured and mutilated souls; and all the tragic and hellish fates that befell good people—and he leaned back, self-satisfied, and waited. Mabel sat her butt down like a good hellhound and gave her master a quick bark of approval.

From a distance, LugWig beheld the Temple and wondered about Gabriel's fate. Well, at least Wig did. Lug was still quite sore about being thwacked on the nose, and even though their scuffle was over, he was thinking about how to deliver his retribution at some later date. Maybe he'd force Wig's holier-than-thou head into the next tree trunk that they came across. *Yeah! That's a good idea!* considered Lug.

They were actually sitting on their haunches, facing the Temple, and Wig watched with concern, while Lug licked his foreleg and plotted.

"Something's wrong," interrupted Wig.

"Huh?"

"Something's not right at the Temple. It's changed color. It's in a cloud of red haze or something."

"So what. Who cares? Forget about that little twerp. We need to think about us, for once. Hopefully, he's being eaten alive by a wormhole demon. Yeah! That'd fit the crime, eh?"

Wig looked at Lug with exhausted, disbelieving pity, and hoped from deep in his heart that one day Lug would grow up a bit. Just the smallest bit would be enough to give Wig hope.

LugWig stood up, by Wig's desire.

"What are you doing?" squealed Lug.

"We need to check this out," Wig counseled, forcefully.

"NO! NO! Forget about it! I'm not gunna go!"

"We have to go," Wig stated with steely reserve. "We have to go."

Payne was frowning and Mabel was whimpering. No matter the level of intensity of the deep, dark, twisted, evil and hellish phenomenon that Payne manifested and thrust Gabriel's way, the effect upon Gabriel was the same: none whatsoever. Gabriel continued his calm and resolute resistance to the entire evil revue, and even seemed to be gaining strength from the whole affair; like the eye of a storm becoming bigger and stronger, the more chaotically the storm clouds swirled around it.

"This is ridiculous!" Payne shouted to Mabel, over the din of the hellspawn. "I've never seen anything like this! I am *not* amused!"

Mabel yapped a worried yap in reply, hoping not to receive the brunt of Payne's frustrated anger in one form or another.

Her master then suddenly smiled. "Aha! I know what to do."

Mabel's tongue slipped out her mouth in happy anticipation, and her tail wagged excitedly.

Payne then reached behind his back and pulled out a gun. It looked like a cross between a prop from a cheesy science fiction film from the fifties, and a 25¢ drug store water pistol. Upon spotting it though, Mabel became intensely excited, indeed, and was barking like she was starving and about to be fed a plate of piping hot and juicy filet mignon.

"This'll tilt the scales," Payne predicted confidently.

Mabel turned her attention to Gabriel floating calmly in the midst of the maelstrom and shielded her eyes from what was to come.

Payne calmly raised the pistol to eye-level for good aim, squinted tightly, then fired, keeping the trigger down as the small, missile-like bullets shot from the chamber of the gun and exploded upon Gabriel's happy little bubble of peace.

Round upon round slammed into Gabriel's space, exploding on contact into mighty fireballs. In mere seconds, Gabriel was engulfed in a giant ball of fire, obscured from Payne's and Mabel's view by the chaos.

Even Lug couldn't deny that something unsavory was happening at the Temple, now. The reddish glow from before had morphed into a yellow, red, and blue glowing sphere, from which lightening was shooting in all directions—like one of those crazy monster-creating machines from old horror films.

LugWig upped his clip into a frantic run, eager to get a closer look. Upon reaching the edge of the multihued energy sphere, both Lug and Wig stuck their heads through the sphere's surface and were able to see more or less clearly what was transpiring inside.

"My God!" Wig exclaimed, not being heard above the ruckus.

"Shussh!" Lug admonished, and Wig did shush, knowing that their presence must not be known, lest they become soul-meat for the ravenous and evil beings that they now beheld.

Payne fired his last round, then lowered his gun, grinning like a piranha. Mabel was panting happily, but then tilted her head to the side in confusion as the smoke cleared.

"God damn it!" Payne shrieked when he could finally see that his barrage didn't penetrate Gabriel's fortress of solitude any more than a pebble thrown limply would.

"God bloody damn it!" he shrieked again.

Mabel was whimpering constantly now, much as a dog that needs to pee very badly does, desperate to be taken for a walk.

"Well done!" Wig muttered inaudibly under his breath, very proud he was of Gabriel's newfound abilities.

"Okay!" Payne asserted sternly. "I didn't want to have to use this, as I can use this once and never again. But now is the time, obviously, since no one can *ever* escape the clutches of Payne!"

With this, Payne again reached behind his back and presented to a suddenly very fearful and confused Mabel a large missile-like attachment that he meant to mount on the end of his gun. Mabel dropped to her belly and covered her eyes with both paws, whimpering pitifully.

"Fear not," counseled Payne to his nervous companion, "for I know how to use this. We'll be fine."

Wig was scared too, for he'd seen this weapon before.

"Lug!" he whispered. "That's a 45-G SquelchMine TrapeZoider! If he uses that on Gabriel, his essence will be sent into another dimension outside of the multiple dimensions of our temporal space/time, forever! We've got to do something!"

"No we don't!" Lug replied.

What happened next could only seem possible in a fairy tale, but it actually did happen.

Payne attached the 45-G SquelchMine TrapeZoider to the end of his pistol and secured it with a click. He smiled.

Wig's brain then beheld in front of him a trail of energy from his body in an arc to a point intersecting the path of the 45-G missile, on its projected pathway to Gabriel. And he knew beyond a shadow of a doubt exactly what, when, and how to do what he knew was imperative for him to now do.

"Don't do it!" Lug shouted from the pit of his fearful being.

Payne didn't notice Lug's loud missive though as he was focusing on firing the dreaded 45-G accurately into Gabriel's face.

LugWig then sprung from his hidden spot like a cannonball from a catapult. And as Payne's gooey, fleshy finger was pressing down up the trigger of his pistol, from the right side of his peripheral vision came the flying, two-headed sheep. But before he could react, Payne's finger had pressed down sufficiently enough to set the charge flying. And as the dreaded missile left its barrel, LugWig's wool-covered body came into view to intersect it.

As LugWig approached this moment of truth, he opened his mouth and, in midair, took the missile into his gullet. The missile didn't explode, however, but instead it rode through LugWig's digestive track like a bobsled careening down its ice-slippery path.

This only lasted an instant, but it was most painful for LugWig as one might expect. And as the missile was bouncing through LugWig's lower intestine, Wig shifted his body weight in midflight so his butthole was pointed straight at Payne and Mabel. And as what seemed to be preordained to happen did in fact happen: the 45-G shot out of LugWig's butt. And before an astounded Payne could react, it ignited the moment its detonator (located in its tip) touched the forehead of his unbelieving and frozen-in-fear face.

As the 45-G ignited, it produced a purple iridescent ball twelve feet in diameter, big enough to grab Payne and Mabel and all space and time in their immediate vicinity. An instant later, and the purple, shining energy ball contracted to a single, impossibly small point, and all that it contained was sent straight away to another place and time. The remaining fabric of existence was pulled together and healed seamlessly.

When the chaos settled into calm, Gabriel found himself sitting in the hand-chair, inside the Temple, as if none of the ridiculous events of the last few moments had ever occurred, and LugWig was lying on the floor at his feet, writhing in quite obvious pain, apparently dying.

"You bastard," Lug managed to squeak out in agony, using all of his remaining energy to tilt his head Wig's way. "I told you not to do it…"

"I had to…" Wig squeaked back.

Gabriel stepped off the chair, and it melted back down into the floor. He leaned down over LugWig and felt profound compassion and empathy for LugWig's pain, and for the sacrifice that he had just made, for Gabriel's sake.

"I'm sorry," Gabriel managed, his lower lip quivering.

And at that, LugWig began to morph into something else. His two heads melted into one, and his sheep limbs grew in size. In but a moment, it was clear to Gabriel that LugWig was shape-shifting into a human. And as the process completed itself, Gabriel realized with shock, hurt and pain who that human was: lying at his feet, dressed as he remembered him even when he was a small boy, laid his father.

Gabriel's father opened his eyes, gave them a good rub, and managed to sit up, bleary-eyed and confused. He saw Gabriel, and beheld a crying, quivering boy. It only took him a few milliseconds to realize that Gabriel was his son, and he was his father, and with that, he held his arms out in invitation to hug his lost son. Gabriel lurched forward instinctively, and the two shared a long overdue embrace.

Gabriel's father was a stoic man prone to angry outbursts, back when he was alive, anyway, and he carried his thin frame, sharp features and dark, closely-cropped hair like a person haunted. Now, however, he seemed reborn, if not literally. And entirely human, if not actually. Apparently, his stint as a two-headed, schizophrenic sheep taught him an important lesson or two, as it probably would anyone.

There was a thundering interruption from above. A voice boomed down and filled the temple interior with vibration and bright light. A light heavenly choir with harp seemed to resonate with the light.

"What have we here then?" came what one could only assume was the Voice of God. Thing was, he sounded a little peeved.

Instinctively, Gabriel and his father lurched upward into taut standing positions as if soldiers on review. They gave each other grave, unnerved glances.

"So…" God prattled on. "I see here that the two of you have taken some sort of important steps in…uh…" The sound of shuffling paper brought confusion to both Gabriel's and his father's expressions. "Uh…Okay… Hold on a sec…"

More paper shuffling. The heavenly choir droned on behind it, feeling a bit like Muzak in a waiting room.

"Uh, hang on for a moment, won't you?" God seemed a little embarrassed, and Gabriel could hear some muted, animated words, like a person putting their hand over the phone to keep an argument private. God was not amused and seemed to be barking orders at his underlings.

Suddenly: "Right, then! Here it is!" God happily announced.

The light from above sharpened its focus directly onto Gabriel's father, and God continued.

"You, sir, whose given name at birth was and still is Jerry Winston McGregor, have finally completed your stint in the underworld by battling your dark side successfully and finally showing proper love and protection to your only son."

Both Gabriel and his father smiled broadly.

"As a result," added God, "you will be given the key to the kingdom, and have finally been accepted into Heaven. It's a really cool place. I think you'll like it here!"

The focused light beamed from God, then shifted to Gabriel.

"You, little man, whose birth name was and still is Gabriel Ellis McGregor, have completed something important here, I suppose, but I'm not quite sure what..." God's voice trailed off, and you could imagine him adjusting his glasses and reading fine print to figure out what was going on.

Gabriel gave his father a worried look. His father nodded back with confidence. Gabriel relaxed a bit.

"Well, this is unusual and a little embarrassing, but I'm not sure where to put you! It seems we fouled up handling your soul and have made a right mess of things..."

An uncomfortably pregnant pause. More heavenly Muzak. God continued.

"I'm not finding proper documentation...Geez... You're not supposed to be in Hell, are you?"

Gabriel's heart sank to his toes. *Not again?* he bemoaned to himself. Then, he remembered something and pulled a small, tattered piece of paper from his back pocket. He held it in the light, so God could see it.

"What's this then?" God pondered.

A moment later, and God concluded: "Fair enough. That bastard Satan himself has given you proper exit from Hell, so you definitely don't belong there… Hmmmm…Still…Where do you go? This is a toughie!"

Gabriel shifted his posture noticeably, put his hands on his hips, and sighed loudly. God picked up on his lack of patience.

"Relax! Administering souls isn't easy, now!"

Gabriel tapped his left foot in frustration. His father spoke up:

"God?"

"Yes, my son?"

"Can't you send him to heaven with me? We do have a lot of catching up to do."

Gabriel beamed with pride and happiness at the notion.

"Technically, that makes sense," God returned, "but my advisors are whispering something in my ear, here… hold on a sec…"

Gabriel resumed tapping his foot, his expression a slight bit exasperated.

"Okay. Here's the deal. Because we fouled everything up in regard to the handing of your soul, Gabriel Ellis McGregor, we're giving you a choice. My advisors have assured me that this is the fairest deal, lest we be sued."

"Sued?" came Gabriel's father's confused reply.

"Um…Sorry…Just put that idea out of your head, if you don't mind."

God sounded a bit flustered. Gabriel's father gave Gabriel a look of amazement, then added a snickering grin.

"Your choice is, Gabriel Ellis McGregor, that you can either, [A] go to Heaven with your father"—happy smiles all around—"or, [B] return to Earth and your family, as you were, having survived your unfortunate accident in the bathtub."

"Can my father come back too?" Gabriel blurted, excitedly.

"Um, well…No. Sorry. He died fair and square years ago and has done his penance in the underworld and is rightly slated for his entrance into Heaven. No foul-ups there. Sorry."

Gabriel suddenly felt confused and tired and not at all happy. He wanted his entire family together back on Earth. God interrupted:

"Sorry, Gabriel Ellis McGregor. Just can't do it."

Gabriel's father added: "Go back and take care of your mother and your sister, son."

Gabriel became deeply sad, instantly. He just met his father, for all intents and purposes, and he was about to lose him again.

"Do it for me, Gabriel. We'll see each other again, soon enough…"

Gabriel realized that it made perfect sense for him to return, with his father's blessing, to his family and to his life as a kid, but the idea of leaving his father's side was ripping a hole in his heart. He managed to squeak out a stout, manly reply, however.

"Okay..." he muttered.

"Good boy!" replied his father. "We'll see each other soon."

Gabriel's father began to float upward toward his soul's destination. He kept talking. "Before you know it, we'll all be in Heaven...Take care of your mother and your sister!" His voice was starting to fade as he floated further upward. "I love you! Tell your mother and sister that I love them!"

Gabriel watched his father's soul disappear into the heavens with wistful tears in his eyes. His demeanor turned to excitement, however, when he realized that he'd soon be home again, and his otherworldly travails would finally be over.

"Okay, then!" God boomed, shaking Gabriel out of his reverie. "Back to earth it is, then! Wise decision, I think! Good man! Your family will be glad you did it!"

Gabriel too began to float upward. He saw the ground below him shrink quickly, as if viewed from a launching rocket ship.

"Let me leave you with a little token of wisdom," God counseled.

"Everything is an illusion. Nothing is real. Except Love. Love is the only thing that's real. Remember that! Even I am an illusion. Love is the only thing that's truly real!"

The profundity of God's statement electrocuted Gabriel's soul into a wave of bright-light excitement that only deep, undeniable truth can. It resonated so deeply with Gabriel's firmament that he found himself shimmering in a cloud of intense, white energy, as if every molecule of his existence was vibrating at an insanely high frequency. As if he was a high, lovely, transcendent note being played on the most beautiful instrument ever created. And as the note began to fade, Gabriel realized that he was sitting in his bathtub, and Emma was crying at him, scared to her marrow, and holding a wet, round, unknown contraption in both her trembling hands.

BACK HOME

GABRIEL WAS SHOCKED and confused and wet and didn't quite know what to make of what he'd been through. After he calmed down Emma, then dried off from his bath, he was forced to consider that the whole affair was a dream or hallucination of some type, brought on by the electric shock that he had received.

Still, if that's all it was, then, he'd probably be dead because the strength of the electrical current that had coursed through his body was certainly enough to end a person's life, especially that of a little kid like Gabriel.

So Gabriel decided to take the experience on face value and live as if it had actually happened. Every little bit of it. Plus, if he was ever in doubt, all he had to do was look at the strange, small, round piece of technology that Emma had accidentally electrocuted him with when she dunked its fully charged and energetically emanating mechanical visage into Gabriel's bath. It sat on his bedside table now, looking to his mother like just another toy of a smart boy's fascination. It was no longer glowing or showing any signs of life, but Gabriel was convinced that he'd get to the bottom of how it worked with the help of his dad's books, especially now that he had access to his father's computer.

Gabriel had changed his opinion of his sister Emma too. The two of them were in this adventure together: that there could be no doubt. And they were having fun keeping their own, very important secret. Gabriel was now endeavoring to treat Emma with respect and love, instead of thinking of her as an annoyance, and the odd thing was, the moment he started behaving in this new fashion, Emma stopped being annoying, and instead became his new, best (actually, "only," really) confidant. This was an important lesson to Gabriel even if he'd learned nothing else from the whole affair.

He also felt less inclined to demonstrate his intellectual prowess—as he saw it—to his friends and classmates, and noticed there too that his peers seemed more relaxed and accepting of his presence. He was now a little less of a loner.

He thought of his dad a lot, of course, and LugWig visited him in his dreams on a regular basis, counseling him about whatever was bugging him at the time.

Was it really his father in the form of a two-headed sheep, visiting him in the night? Or was it his subconscious communicating with his consciousness in an interesting way? Did it matter? Gabriel began to think not. The effect was the same. Gabriel Ellis McGregor was now, it seemed, a genuinely good boy...